Advance praise for Katey Schultz's

FLASHES OF WAR

"This is a brilliant, unsettling, and disturbingly beautiful book…Writing of this degree of commitment and integrity is living evidence of the power of fiction to tell the truth about reality."

> – Joydeep Roy-Bhattacharya, author of *The Watch*

"Katey Schultz has written an amazing book. What emerges from these stories is a chorus of voices—American, Afghan, Iraqi—and this chorus enlarged my sense of the experience of a war that has defined an American decade. *Flashes Of War* is the work of a bold, ambitious, and brilliant young author who is writing stories few others in American fiction have really yet tackled."

> – Doug Stanton, author of New York Times Bestsellers *Horse Soldiers* and *In Harm's Way*

"…precise, finely wrought metaphors and evocative images that linger long after you turn the page."

> – *Fiction Writers Review*

"The title of this fine book may lead us to believe we'll see the war in the Middle East in tiny, fragmentary bursts of the sort that come to us in nightmares, and this book indeed bursts in small ways throughout, in tight narratives, in arresting images, in brilliant searches into the distresses of the human heart, but *Flashes of War* is so much more than that. This is a book about the whole war, the soldiers on both sides, the civilians on both sides, the consequences for everybody involved before, during, and after. This book, maybe more effectively than any in a long time, pleads with humanity to end war once and for all. Read this book, and seek peace."

> – Mike Magnuson, author of *Lummox, The Evolution of a Man*

FLASHES OF WAR

Short Stories by Katey Schultz

FLASHES OF WAR

Short Stories by Katey Schultz

Apprentice House
Loyola University Maryland
Baltimore, Maryland

First Edition

Printed in the United States of America
Paperback ISBN: 978-1-934074-85-5
EBook ISBN: 978-1-934074-37-4

Cover design by: Samantha Garvey

Published by Apprentice House

Apprentice House
Loyola University Maryland
4501 N. Charles Street
Baltimore, MD 21210
410.617.5265 • 410.617.2198 (fax)
www.apprenticehouse.com
info@apprenticehouse.com

CREDITS

"That Sunday Morning Feeling," "Checkpoint," and "Pressin' the Flesh" published in *Future Cycle Flash* and the *Future Cycle Flash Anthology*.

"Just the Dog & Me" published in *Flash: The International Short-Short Story Magazine*.

"WIA," "MIA," and "KIA" published in *War, Literature and the Arts: An International Journal of the Humanities*.

"While the Rest of America's at the Mall" shortlisted for Fish Publishing International One-Page Fiction Prize.

"Into Pure Bronze" (published as "Kabul Stadium") in *Talking River Review*.

"Getting Perspective" published in *Connotations*.

"Homecoming" published in *Dunes Review*.

"Amputee" published in *Ars Medica*.

"While the Rest of America's at the Mall," "With the Burqa," and "Just the Dog & Me" published as limited edition letterpressed broadsides by Gold Quoin Press in collaboration with the students of Bradley University.

"Home on Leave" published in *Hot Metal Bridge*.

"KIA" reprinted in *Flash: The International Short-Short Story*

Magazine (England).

"While the Rest of America's at the Mall," "With the Burqa" and "The Ghost of Sanchez" reprinted in *Afghan Scene Magazine* (Afghanistan).

"The Quiet Kind" was reprinted in *Serving House Journal*.

ACKNOWLEDGEMENTS

I extend my sincerest gratitude to the following organizations, their staffs, and board members who supported the completion of this book through fellowships, residencies, and teaching opportunities: Interlochen Center for the Arts (especially Mika Perrine and Matthew Wiliford); North Carolina Humanities Council along with Weymouth Center for the Arts and Humanities; Jentel Foundation; Fishtrap (especially Barbara Dills) and Imnaha Writers' Retreat; The Warehouse Sessions at Studio 7; Madroño Ranch: A Center for Writing, Art, and the Environment; Virginia Center for the Creative Arts; The Island Institute of Sitka, Alaska; 49 Alaska Writing Center; and Prairie Center of the Arts.

Several people reviewed early drafts of the manuscript for accuracy. I would like to thank Shannon Huffman Polson (Captain, US Army Aviation, 1993-2001) for assistance understanding military branches and divisions of power, as well as use of Denali Arts 229; Sergeant First Class Warren Bockhol for weapons accuracy and his descriptions of a Forward Operating Base; Karen Button (former war correspondent) for answering countless questions and steering me toward resources on Middle Eastern culture; and Doug Stanton for *Horse Soldiers* and his support of this work. I would also like to thank my agent, John Sibley Williams, and my copyeditor, Mike Magnuson.

I owe a debt of gratitude to the faculty of the Pacific University MFA in Writing Program, most specifically Judy Blunt (for verbs), Pete Fromm (for teaching me to relax), Claire Davis (for precision, passion, and abandon), Jack Driscoll (because one sentence announces the possibility of the next), and Shelley Washburn (for encouragement). And to two of my earliest creative writing teachers, Ms. Wood and Professor Hashimoto, who planted the seeds without which this would never have grown.

Likewise, those priceless writing friends who have swapped stories with me, offered invaluable critiques, and generally have made the writing life a life worth living—endless appreciation for Anne-Marie, Britt, Cam, Compton, Kyle, Mendy, Mary, Rosie, and Wesley. With regard to final revisions and the good work of digging in: Ester, Brendan, Jenny, and the fine state of Alaska.

I spent 31 out of 36 months traveling across the United States while I wrote *Flashes of War*. Strangers hosted me for dinner; community members shared their homes; local arts organizations sponsored readings and events; students engaged during class; friends of friends reached out and made me feel welcome; colleagues accepted me; fellow artists shared their work and inspired my own; and perhaps most importantly, supporters new and old encouraged my journey without question. Their faith in what at many times felt like an impossibly long road ultimately helped me find my way home. Without their support, these stories could not have been written.

Last but not least, thanks to the dependables: THE CLAW, Bob Dylan, Gus, and Duckie.

This book is dedicated to my parents,
who believed in me before I knew what belief was.

Elizabeth Buss Schultz

&

William Henry Schultz

CONTENTS

WHILE THE REST OF AMERICA'S AT THE MALL

It's not quite sniper fire, but it isn't random either. The hajis so much as hear me think, and they start gunning the water from their position on the bridge, bullets raining like a Carolina downpour. They can't see me in the dark, so I toss a balled-up T-shirt far as I can toward enemy fire to mess with their thinking. They aim right for it, the shirt lurching like a live wire while I dip underwater and start swimming the opposite direction. By the time I've crawled up the banks of the Darya-ye Konar and radioed the airstrike on their exact location, the hajis are still standing there, shooting that shirt all the way to the Indus River.

Dark-swimming is my gig this tour. Navy SEALS. You'd never believe me, but the underwater night goggles make this place look like the tropics. Bullets glitter through the water in slow-mo, little Hershey's Kisses moving in silver arcs the way I remember Savannah tossing them to me on her fourth birthday. "It's raining kisses, Daddy," she sang. She made up the tune and it's almost a joke now, trying to think of the last time I made up a song for no particular reason.

Any second now, that bridge will sizzle, and Spalding will crack some joke about the Konar looking more like haji soup, then LT will pluck that damn tea tree toothpick out of his mouth and nod and say, "Good work, son." So corny it could be from the movies, and I wish this was, all of us busting drug convoys 50 klicks north of Kabul, while the rest of America's at the mall.

WITH THE BURQA

With the burqa, it was like this: the world came at me in apparitions, every figure textured by the mesh filter in front of my eyes. In a city with so much death, it was easy to believe half of the people I saw were ghosts. Women sat like forgotten boulders along the sidewalks in Kabul. We begged. We prayed.

Now, wearing the burqa is a choice. Without it, the sun is so bright that when I walk it feels like swimming through sticky, yellow air. I can see clearly, but there's nothing left of my city to look at. A missile that didn't detonate sleeps like a gigantic baby in my garden, cradled in a ten-foot crater of dirt and rubble. There used to be a brick wall around my family's home. My father built that wall. Now, my father is gone, and the wall is gone, and even the tools for restoring the wall have been looted from our doorstep.

One night, I dream that the missile takes root. The garden groans and stretches, growing rounds of ammunition and grenades. In the dream, the entire neighborhood comes to harvest from my weapons cache. I wander through the rows of weaponry, tugging bullets by their brass tips. They fall into my palms like succulent berries. The grenades are more difficult, but my touch is soft. I set them in my satchel like fresh eggs and carry them to the market where servicemen from the base are having a holiday.

They come to my booth reluctantly at first, then hungrily when they realize the weapons have grown from the earth. Here's a bullet for the sergeant who pestered my children in the middle of the night. A handful for his team members, the way they looked at us like something to be pitied. And the grenades? Those are for the pilot who dropped the missile on my house. Watch how trustingly he takes the satchel, hugging it like a new parent. When everything is sold, I leave the market and slowly walk home. I hear the pop and whir of bullets first, then the grenades explode. I don't have to turn around to see what disaster looks like.

When I wake, the sun is a ball of flame arcing over my city. There's no escape from its heat. I reach for my burqa and cover myself once more. It's damp and dark in here, just like the grave where my father's bones have turned to dust.

HOME ON LEAVE

One minute Bradley's at the dinner table shoveling homemade rhubarb pie into his mouth, and the next he's tearing down the driveway in his Ford Ranger, clean Arkansas air slapping him across the face with that unmistakable feeling of home. It's been ten months and twenty-three days, but who's counting? Not Bradley. Not anymore. Not since he kicked off his combat boots, hugged his mom, and split a six-pack with his old man. Not since now, miles clicking along the county road as the Ranger pushes seventy, and Bradley tries to make it to his brother Jared's house in under ten, like before.

Before. His dad warned him about that. Bradley hardly listened. What could a gristmill manager teach an eighteen-year-old Army recruit gearing up for 21st Century warfare? But sure enough, the advice whistled in Bradley's ears as he rounded the corner near the gas station and turned right over Little Patmos Creek. "There's a before and after, son," his dad had told him. "The trick is not getting stuck fantasizing about either one." It made no sense at the time and didn't make any more sense now. Bradley still owed the Army three years. "After" was hardly a thought.

Out past the beam of the Ranger's headlights, past the two-block town of Patmos, the hillsides of Hempstead County bristled in the early winter air. Before he enlisted, Bradley hadn't seen much further than that. But tonight, tomorrow night, heck, for the next two weeks—who cared that he was small-town? That he wasn't even old enough to buy Bud Light? He'd been to Iraq and back. Sure, he was out of harm's way most of his deployment, replacing gaskets and fixing flats as a wheeled vehicle mechanic on a forward operating base south of Tikrit, but who knew? Nobody back home had heard of *fobbits*, the derogatory name combat soldiers used for the likes of Bradley.

At the party—a welcome home thrown by his brother—he'd expected the backslapping and WMD jokes that came later that evening. Even the uncertain gazes from folks who probably thought he'd been killing Iraqi citizens. What he hadn't expected was this: the soft-eyed looks all the girls gave him, the respectful nods from guys he didn't even know. In the ten seconds it took Bradley to hop out of his truck and walk across Jared's yard, the entire party's eyes found him. He felt their attention like a shot of adrenaline. He'd been places since graduation. He must know things now; he might even be traumatized. And brave. Surely he was very, very brave.

"Bradley!" Jared took the porch steps in one leap and rammed his chest into his brother's. "Man, you're solid as a rock! Look at you!" He pounded Bradley's arm a few times and jostled him.

"It's good to see you! Thanks for this." Bradley waved at the porch filled with partiers, plastic keg cups in their hands. A few friends he hadn't seen since graduation waved back. Most folks, though, he didn't even recognize.

Jared slung his arm over Bradley's shoulders and walked him toward the porch. "Are you kidding? You're all anybody talks about in Patmos these days. Hometown hero."

"Really?" Bradley asked.

"I'll bet you the crack of my ass you'll be in the paper next week. Home on leave. Patmos' very own." They ambled up the porch steps, the crowd parting for them as they moved. "Great citizens of Patmos, Arkansas," Jared bellowed. "Private Bradley Coates, a.k.a RAMBO." A cheer shot up from the porch, a few dogs barking at the outburst. "Welcome home, little bro. We fuckin' love you. Don't we fuckin' love him?" Another cheer.

The partiers chanted, "Speech, speech, speech, speech" and stomped their feet over shaky joists.

Bradley froze. Even as a star wrestler in high school he hadn't been singled out, not like this. What could he possibly give a speech about? In the Army, nobody looked at him dead-on unless it was some head-tripper doling out put-downs just because Bradley hadn't fired his M4 since Fort Jackson. Fobbits were all the same. Just a bunch of laborers, holing up inside the wire. Heck, Bradley could have spent the last ten months working for Jiffy Lube.

"I only have one thing to say," he said and smiled in mock profundity. If his big brother had taught him anything, it was not to lose the moment, even if he had to fake it. "Where's the beer?"

Another cheer roared from the crowd, twenty red cups thrust his direction. Bradley looked at the eager faces shining beneath the porch light, their teeth clacking as if to say, *Take mine! No, take mine!* He grabbed the closest beer and slugged it down, and the last gulp splashed onto his coat.

Toward midnight, Bradley felt his shoulders pressed too tightly into his coat, the plastic cup almost miniature in his palm. "You're still growing!" his mother had written in those early care packages overflowing with Oreos and beef jerky. Bradley felt babied by this, though his mother guessed right. He was constantly hungry. Yes, from growing, but more from the long shifts and all that weightlifting he'd done to kill the boredom in between. It didn't matter now. He was home on leave. He could have stuffed-crust pizza delivered to his doorstep at midnight if he wanted.

Music howled from somewhere inside the house. A small crowd huddled around a campfire out back. Bradley emptied his cup again and aimed for the keg, a little swagger in his stride. A petite brunette fussed with the pump, turning toward him as he approached.

"Sonya?" Bradley asked. He hadn't meant to sound so surprised. She moved away his sophomore year.

"Bradley!" she said and gave him a hug. "Good timing. Can you figure this out?"

He took her cup and set it next to his along the railing. Sonya Winters had never given him a hug before. She'd barely been able to remember his name, always referring to him as "Jared's little brother" or "the one on the wrestling team." The keg was empty, but another waited. He tapped it and cleared the foam. While he worked, Sonya explained herself.

"My parents split, like two months after we left Patmos," she said. "It sucks for my dad. I feel bad for him. But mom and me came back here. I'm at the community college now. I have to take pre-calc again. Can you believe it? Slit my throat."

"Here." Bradley handed Sonya her cup.

"Thanks," she said. "You look good."

"Huh?" He inspected himself for a moment: ratty Converse and extra long Levi's, a white cotton tee sticking out the bottom of his Carhartt jacket. He still hadn't been able to shake the thought that he looked underdressed. Civilian clothes felt useless compared to DCUs.

He looked at her. She seemed tired. "Well, cheers!" he said, finally.

"Cheers!" She smiled, and when Bradley tipped his cup to hers, she kissed him on the cheek.

He blushed, but turned away and walked into the house. Sonya

Winters. She'd always been a flirt. Bradley remembered when Jared took her to prom, the way he bragged about her for weeks afterwards. "Tits like another planet," he'd told Bradley, gesturing with cupped palms. "And she laughs when she comes, like she's being tickled. Biggest fucking turn on."

Girls like Sonya weren't in Bradley's league then, not that Jared hadn't tried his best to set things up for his little brother. By the time Bradley got to high school, Jared's reputation had carved a path for him whether he wanted it or not. It got him through the basics of small town sex with girls everybody knew but with nobody Bradley felt particularly nostalgic about. Where Jared had relationships, Bradley fumbled with dates and dances until sports became more manageable than girls. Where Jared had a shoe-in at the County Extension after earning his Associate's, Bradley could hardly sit through Chem class, always fidgety in a chair. Yet both men were tirelessly loyal—to each other, to friends, even to two-block Patmos. The comparison with his brother, had Bradley made the connection, might have been something like two sides of the same coin. Bonded in material, no doubt, but depending on who you asked, one always appeared in the shadow of the other.

Tonight, Bradley felt bolstered by all the attention. The beer helped. The cool night air helped. The sound of friends, instead of generators, helped, too. He walked to the kitchen to fill his cup with water. He needed to pace himself if he wanted to remember how well all this was going. Before he turned from the sink, he felt a pair of eyes on his back.

"Big night, soldier." It was a male voice, flat-toned—not local.

Bradley heard more feet shuffle into the room. Two men, judging by the sounds of their boots. That made three, total. He tried to ignore the way his stomach tightened, his knees locking into hyperextension. The stranger's tone had a tinny familiarity to

9

it, as though a squad of bloodied combat troops had just delivered their broken down Humvee and glared at him for looking so goddamn clean. More than once, he'd heard, "After you're done baking muffins, see if you can't get around to fixing our rig." Bradley exhaled and turned around. He'd guessed right about the men in the kitchen—three of them standing there, a little stupid and slow-looking at the end of a long night. But he hadn't guessed about the bag of crystal meth the stranger tossed onto the kitchen counter, or the tattoo that said INFIDEL poking out of his half-unbuttoned flannel. That's what insurgents called American soldiers. That's what almost every tip-of-the-spear troop he'd met on base in Tikrit had inked somewhere on their bodies.

"You've been there, too, huh?" Bradley asked. He leaned his back against the counter, a kitchen island with salsa and chips stood between them. He could eat all that and then some, maybe root around for cheese and make microwave nachos. But not now. Not with this soldier and his two buddies filling the kitchen, their stares unflinching.

"Hell yeah, I've been there. Twice," the stranger said. "Left my leg there, too." He stepped around the island and tugged at his pant leg, revealing a high-tech prosthesis from the knee down, a fake foot filling out the toes of his shoe.

"Jesus," Bradley said.

The stranger laughed loudly. "Look at you, whiter than a fuckin' ghost. What are you? Giving blowjobs over there on base all day?"

The others joined and their laughter invaded the kitchen. Bradley stepped around the island, toward the stranger. It wouldn't take much. A sideswipe to the guy's bad leg would send him to the floor.

Jared strolled into the kitchen, Sonya in tow. "What'd I miss, Taylor?" he asked.

"Nothing yet. But stick around and you might see Mr. Welcome Home try and get tough."

Just then, Bradley lunged, ducking fast beneath Taylor's arms and ramming him into the pantry door. What would have been a take down and two points back in high school was now just an awkward moment, Bradley the star fool. Taylor looked down at the boy wrapped around his rib cage and gave a chuckle.

"Well, how about that," he said.

Bradley angled his weight into Taylor and felt the hinge on his prosthesis start to give. And as though it were as easy as shaking hands, Taylor slid one meaty arm underneath Bradley's chin, securing a head lock. The other, he used in a guillotine—both illegal moves in any high school match, but who said anything about playing straight? Bradley's head throbbed, his field of vision suddenly speckled into fading stars.

"Ah, relax," Jared said.

Taylor eased up, and Bradley slowly backed out of the position. Seamlessly then, he felt Taylor's thick palms grip his shoulders and flip him around into a full nelson. Jared laughed then, too, seeing his brother's face, cheeks flushed and veins throbbing along his temples.

"What the fuck?" Bradley squeezed out.

"He's just messing with you, bro. Isn't that right?"

"That's right," Taylor said and released his grip. "Just like Iraq. A little hand-to-hand to keep things real."

"Right," Bradley said, stepping away and popping his neck. He had a mind to flee but it was his party, wasn't it? He leaned against the kitchen island to steady himself. As he rubbed his hands along his throat, he felt a small impression where the buttons on Taylor's shirt had gouged into his flesh like a tiny, faked bullet hole.

"You bring what I asked?" Jared said.

"Sure as shit," Taylor said. "And the high's almost as good as a fire fight."

The others settled around the kitchen table, Sonya sitting on Jared's knee. His brother took a hit from the pipe, electric white smoke crackling into the air. As if reading Bradley's mind, Jared exhaled and looked at his brother.

"Don't worry, kid. It's only every once in a while." He smiled, then passed the pipe to Sonya.

Kid. The word didn't sit well anymore. Kids didn't enlist in the Army. Kids didn't have keggers thrown in their honor, local papers touting their military accomplishments, strangers in airports thanking them for their service. Kids weren't hometown heroes, but maybe Bradley wasn't, either. He'd certainly been shown as much a few minutes ago, wrapped in Taylor's death grip. He shoved his way out the back door and wandered into the yard. The night felt cool and damp, as if on the edge of a rainstorm. How long had Jared been hanging around guys like that? He'd acted so casual. Then again, he hadn't heard Taylor's crack about blowjobs—or had he? Bradley breathed deeply and kicked his feet along the top of the grass. No dust. No camel spiders. Just that sweet air laced with the sideways hint of a norther.

A few minutes passed and he heard the front door open and close, then a car pulling out of the driveway. *Fucking infidel,* he thought. Weren't they all fighting in the same war? Choking on the same sand? Guzzling the same chlorinated water that gave everybody the shits? "You'll make a good team player," a recruitment officer had told Bradley when he looked over his high school transcripts, noting the weight training credits and sports accolades. But as a wrestler he was the one in charge, long seconds between the ref's whistle to start and end each match something like a buzz for Bradley as he maneuvered ankle picks and duck-unders, always quicker than his opponents. Teammates hollered from the sidelines, but those seconds in between were all Bradley's—from the instant decisions he made locking arms with the other guy, to those rare moments he found himself pressed into the mat, body contorted into passivity, when he knew he'd been beat. That was gone now, and though Bradley had moments of cleverness on the roller board underneath a Humvee, wrenches and bolts in hand, those victories were quiet. Smaller. Hardly noticed in the great machinery of war.

Sonya's laughter cut through the night air, the sound emanating from somewhere back inside. Bradley stumbled to the edge of the lawn and unzipped to take a piss. He could crash on the couch downstairs, but, no. He wanted his own bed. He zipped up and started walking down the driveway.

"Hey, hold on a sec," a voice called.

"Who's there?" Bradley saw a figure squatting near the shrubs by the mailbox, just beyond the reach of the porch lights.

"It's Ashleigh," she said and stood. "Sorry. The bathroom was locked. Can I get a ride? I'm just in the apartments above the gas station."

"Yeah, sure," he said. "I'm Bradley."

"I know," she said. "Nice party."

She looked at him, her light skin visible through the darkness. Her blond bangs were trimmed to just above her eyebrows. A few hairs caught in her thick mascara. She was older. Twenty-one? Twenty-two? They hadn't gone to school together, he knew that much.

"You ready? That's me over there." He pointed to the Ranger.

"Yeah," she said. "You good to drive?"

"Good enough." Bradley shrugged. He hoped it was true.

Minutes later, they stood awkwardly at the bottom of the steps behind the gas station, sharing a cigarette. If this had been Jared's moment, they might not have made it out of the truck, windows steaming in the damp starlight. But enough of Jared. Enough of folks thinking they knew what it meant to go to Iraq. War played out awkwardly, rarely as planned. Bradley's war might be fought in tiny moments inside the wire, but it was still war. It wasn't his fault nobody else could see that.

"It's weird being back," he said. He shifted his weight from side to side, gravel crunching underfoot.

"I bet."

"Kinda makes high school look like a cake walk." As soon as he said it he regretted it, that kid in him always creeping around the edges, making it impossible for anyone to take him seriously. He glanced at Ashleigh and noted the way her lips curled around the cigarette filter as she took another drag. She seemed caught up in something else. If she took him for a kid, she wasn't showing it.

"So?" she asked. "What's it like over there?"

Bradley shook his head. "Nobody's asked me that all night."

She took the last drag and crushed the cigarette beneath her sneakers. "Well, you don't have to say nothin'." She reached for his hands. He felt the cold metal of her watch with the edge of his fingers and imagined how delicately she might remove it before going to sleep. Then he thought of her in bed, himself with her. She smelled like cigarettes and breath mints, but Bradley suspected if he got closer, she'd smell different. He may be walking around without a combat badge, but surely there were some things he could still do right. He slid his arms around her waist and they swayed together, beer tilting the Arkansas sky.

Inside, they stumbled over clothing, the nightstand. Bradley had been right. She smelled like sweetened citrus. The softest thing he'd touched in almost a year. A few minutes into it, he bit her nipples too hard, and she let out a tiny yelp. He made a game of it—gentle kisses all over her body like a thousand apologies and when they finally did finish, Bradley nodded off, the muscles in his body relaxed so thoroughly his joints turned to jelly.

He woke just before dawn, the security light from the gas station angling into Ashleigh's apartment. He got dressed and pulled a chair over to the window. When he reached to slide it open a few inches, Ashleigh woke up.

"Whatchya doin'?" she asked

"Here," he said and took a drag from a cigarette and handed it to her.

"Thanks." She sat up slowly. "What time is it?"

"Dunno. Five?"

Ashleigh took a drag and handed the smoke back to him. He tapped the ash out the window. Outside, the warming sky still held a hint of darkness, trying to outgrow the night before.

"God, my head," she said.

"I'll get you some water."

"No. You don't have to."

But Bradley was already up, muscled body walking toward her bathroom. He emerged a moment later with a plastic cup. He watched her drink, the way her throat stretched long and smooth as she raised her chin. "I gotta go," he said.

Ashleigh set the empty cup on her dresser. "K." She leaned forward and kissed him, her tongue thick and cool from the tap water.

"Can I come by sometime?"

"Yeah," she said. "I'm around."

He drove home slowly, noticing frost across the pastures, a few shallow ditches iced over. Sunrise in Iraq always looked apocalyptic, the horizon announcing itself in fireball red, heat sizzling through the dusty air and warming each day much too quickly. Bradley rolled his window down and let his arm stretch into the morning air. It felt crisp, invigorating. Enough to make each moment seem fresh.

He let himself in quietly, the house humming its gentle noise. The refrigerator. The PC. Muffled voices from a TV left on in the back room. It sounded symphonic to Bradley, almost dream-like. Jared would stop by later, no doubt, probably with another grand adventure planned. Maybe Bradley would stay in this time. Or take the truck on a long drive, radio humming local country. He took off his coat and walked into the kitchen. Leftover rhubarb pie waited for him on the counter.

MY SON WANTED A
NOTEBOOK

How can I tell you this? My son Anoosah worked in a sweatshop weaving rugs. This was during the good time—after the Taliban but before everything got worse again. He worked ten hours, six days a week. His small, brown fingertips looked as blistered and cracked as the streets of downtown Kabul. Still, each day he came home. He kissed my cheeks. He played the games that young boys play, and when he ran, he moved as freely as a cloud.

Anoosah earned two dollars a month. We bought barley and figs. We could only do this sometimes. Other times, I stole from the farmers at the bazaar, stuffing corn and cucumbers into my clothing. Once, Anoosah tried to pillage a nearby hen house. The owner found him sitting on the floor, coddling the hens, their warm, ruffled feathers like nothing he had ever felt. The man took pity and gave Anoosah some eggs, but only after he earned them by cleaning out the coop. "Like silk," Anoosah told me later. "Holding those hens felt like holding bags of silk."

My husband's feet were crushed in the rubble from an American missile in the early attacks. The same people who hurt him later helped him, and so he lived. He uses crutches while we wait for his prosthesis. It's been four months. He sleeps all day. He survived, but the only part that's still alive is his anger. He says his country is nothing if he cannot feel the earth beneath his feet.

A new school opened for women. There were business classes, driving instructions, and lessons on self-care. I got permission to attend and walked there every day. We tried lipstick. Learned basic English. They even gave us lunch. One of the teachers fitted me for eyeglasses, and my handwriting improved.

I told Anoosah everything so he could learn as well. He wanted a notebook of his very own—a small luxury—so I sent him to the shops. I had a voucher from the school for just these kinds of things. He ran out the door, stuffing the voucher into his pockets. He would be able to tell stories and let me write them down for him. He could make sketches of the hills and show them to his father. "Get the biggest one you can," I said. "We'll fill every page!"

The explosion happened a few blocks from the store. I heard it from our home and didn't worry. These things still happened sometimes, though this one was loud and close. My husband pushed himself out of bed and crawled across the kitchen to our front door. "Anoosah," he said and grabbed his crutches and lifted himself up. There was no way to do this quickly, and he wouldn't let me help. He wrangled out the door and onto the street. He hadn't been outside in months. First one crutch, then the other, a sort of hop-heaving motion from one rubber tip of the crutches to the next. I walked next to him as he teetered, a building with no foundation. One block later he collapsed. That's when we saw it.

The car bomb must have gone off at the wrong time, because the driver was a smoking statue, one foot still on the brake, the other sticking out the open door and touching the sidewalk in mock escape. His burning hand looked glued to the door handle.

Limp bodies encircled the flaming car like petals around the center of a flower. How can I tell you this? My son wanted a notebook. He wanted a notebook, and he was killed.

POO MISSION

1st Squad was bedded down in a firm house inside Fallujah. Our worst day of fighting and more casualties than we even knew at that point. But the block was secure, and we had men on watch from rooftop to sidewalk. I had to take a dump, and the only safe place was the building we were sleeping in.

I elbowed my buddy on the floor next to me. "Yo, Holden, you awake?"

"I'm either awake, or I'm dead."

"I gotta take a shit."

Right away, Holden made a big deal of the whole thing. "Freyer's on a poo mission," he announced. Most of the guys were awake anyway, a chorus of chuckles erupting from the moonlit room.

Ruiz said, "He's droppin' the kids off at the pool!"

Caldwell said, "He's takin' the Browns to the Super Bowl!"

Fitz said, "He's unleashing the bomb on Hiroshima!"

"Yeah, and all your moms can't wait to watch me do it," I told them.

We got up and Holden followed me down the dark hallway, broken glass and busted rocks crunching beneath our boots. My ears were ringing, but other than that, the city sounded eerily quiet. I didn't like it one bit. We reached the end of the hall and saw three doors, all shot up.

"Go in the middle one," Holden said. "That's where the dead muj is. I dare you to shit on his face."

"Hell no," I said. "I don't want any muj watching me take a dump, dead or alive." I chose the entrance on the left and walked into the room. The whole place felt like a haunted house with bad ju-ju. Only hours beforehand, this room held a weapons cache for the terrorists trying to keep a stronghold in the city. There weren't any windows, so I clicked on my headlamp and cleared a place to squat. Bullet shells, hypodermic needles, and busted up chairs littered the floor. A rug lay in the corner, stained with blood. Holden waited for me on the other side of the door.

After a few minutes, I heard him light a cigarette.

"Freyer?" he said.

"What?"

"If we make it back, don't tell Maria about the smoking, okay?" He meant if we make it back to Bozeman, where we're both from. We still had two months.

"Man, she should just be happy you're alive," I said.

"Try telling her that," he said. "It's being pregnant. She's fussy about my health now."

I pulled my pants back up and joined him in the hallway. "In that case," I said, "You'd better let me help you with those; for your health and all."

He smiled and tossed me a smoke.

When we got back to the main room, most of the guys were asleep. I could hear Ruiz snoring, and right next to him lay Sergeant Fisher, twitching away in some sort of half sleep. It's an odd thing, seeing your squad so vulnerable like that. They almost looked like strangers—my brothers, my fellow Marines—the way the moon cast a blue light across their bodies. It made them look holy. More than anything, it made them look dead.

REFUGEE

I took my family, and we did what we were told, leaving our house in Fallujah before the second U.S.-led assault. I paid all my money and one basket of food to a cab driver outside the city. He took us as far as our money would go, about seven miles from the al-Hadrha district of Bagdhad. We walked the rest of the way, my wife and two daughters, plus three satchels of belongings that I slung over my back and carried like a camel. I remember feeling the sun warm my shoulders and the taste of dust kicked up along the road. Some days, it felt as though those were the only things left untouched in Iraq: ceaseless heat and tiny particles of the past that could survive any method of warfare.

I heard Doctors Without Borders had set up a camp in al-Hadrha for families like ours. I didn't know who they were or why they would come, but they took us in. We stayed in pole tents with thousands of others—all of this in a district already as crowded as a rug factory. Volunteers served small meals three times a day. Others showed us how to set up tents for families that kept coming. We raised walls, hammered stakes, and secured door flaps all without speaking each other's language. It didn't matter. The work needed doing. We did it together. The city sang around us— sometimes air raids, other times the ritual calls to prayer.

Within a week, my wife found sewing work in Bagdhad. During the daytime, tents were only for the sick or elderly so my daughters played outside. Without any schools, gangs of youth loitered between rows of tents. One afternoon, an elderly woman died, and a small crowd of orphan boys took her santoor to entertain themselves with music. They danced and clapped, unashamed of their thievery. Other times, the gangs grew restless and taunted each other or dared girls in no-good games. A crippled teen played on my daughters for sympathy, showing them the stump of his contorted left arm, the fleshy stub where his elbow should have been. When Salia came to find me, she said, "That place, father. He's showing Mishar that place in his pants." I found them in a partially collapsed tent, the cripple's pants unzipped, and Mishar with her hands over her face, crying for what she had seen. I shoved the cripple and kicked the rest of the tent down, leaving him trapped to fend for himself.

Each night inside the tents, men and women wept openly. The wounded slept alongside the healthy. Families argued like bleating goats. One time, a man next to me pounded his fists into his cot repeatedly, refusing to stop. It took four of us to brace his arms behind his back. He looked old and failing, his breath hot and stale on my face. "Yalla! Yalla!" he kept shouting. He wanted to go back. He wanted to fight and protect his home. Didn't we all?

Seven months later, families were allowed to go back. We rode together in a convoy of U.S. Marines. Those men looked indestructible, and yet I knew—we all knew—that the fight in our city had been their hardest yet. I worried for my fellow Fallujahns who stayed behind. We moved slowly along the road and part of me wondered if the convoy was a farce, if the Fallujah I had always known would be completely erased from the Earth.

It took almost fourteen hours to re-enter the city. A fence encircled the perimeter with only three secured gates for thousands of Fallujahns. But these were my people! I felt certain we could thrive again. In line together, we prayed for a new time of peace. I could hardly stand the waiting. I wanted to see my beloved city again, the city of mosques. I could almost taste our famous kabobs and hear vendors singing their prices into the streets. The only blessing while we waited was reuniting with friends we hadn't seen since the invasion. Malik the butcher. Hakim the street vendor. Uday the chai boy. Little slices of our neighborhood returning home like so many migrating birds. Almost as many were missing: Mohammed, Jamail, Abida the barber with the funny Western moustache.

Finally, we neared the gate. I peered through a ticket window and spotted half a dozen soldiers and shelf after shelf of hardware. It sounded like a swarm of electronic flies, beeping and humming in a generator-powered cacophony. The Marines took our daughters first, and pressed their tiny fingertips onto a curious electronic pad. Then they took profile photos and bantered with a translator about our names and street address. Next, they scanned our eyes and turned the images into code. Finally, they led us, exhausted and thirsty, over to a waiting area along the fence. Already, elders fainted in the sun. When the Marines tried to help, their boss came out and hollered at them to stop.

Thirty minutes later, we received biometric badges. "Welcome to the 21st Century," the Marine said. A translator repeated in Arabic. "If you have nothing to hide, you have nothing to worry about. These identification cards can't be misplaced. They're your only pass for this gate. They give you permission to enter your neighborhood. You're prohibited anywhere else. If you lose your cards, you're suspect. If you disobey the boundaries, you're considered hostile."

I stuffed the cards into my breast pocket. The girls could hardly move, so I carried Salia on my back, her tiny brown legs flopping as we walked. When we got to our block, I knew immediately we should not have come. The wall surrounding our small apartment lay crushed into hunks of jagged concrete and stone. The entire roof had been cleanly peeled away, as though someone lifted jam off the top of a pastry. Crooked spires of rebar poked into the sky where our second story bedrooms used to be. I made my family wait in the street while I ducked beneath a crumbling archway and into the remains of our kitchen.

Alone amidst the rubble, I thought about the old man from the tents at al-Hadhra, the one who couldn't be quieted. I curled my fists and pounded, till my knuckles bled into the stone. I would have to face my family empty-handed. To tell them we had nothing, that the tents at al-Hadrha offered more than our very own home. I thrashed and kicked, and the ID cards tumbled from my pocket onto the floor. They shone brightly against the dark rubble. I could still smell the fresh plastic lining each card, a toxic omen for the new Fallujah.

INTO PURE BRONZE

Now that schools are open again and there's government and voting, we spend our days inside reciting numbers and studying legendary Afghans: our first king, Ahmed Shah Durrani; or the martyr Massoud, an anti-Soviet fighter killed by Al Qaeda; and our latest hero, Rohollah Nikpai, Olympic Bronze Medalist in taekwondo. Kabul Stadium even has new grass in anticipation of Nikpai's welcome party.

Sometimes, our schoolteacher turns to the blackboard, and my friend Hadir and I thrust leopard fists into the air, saluting Nikpai. When she snaps to look at us, we sit on our hands and stare at our ledgers, pretending. We are thirteen, oldest in the class, so the other boys don't point or tell. When the teacher turns again, we roll our eyes and snicker. The day goes faster this way, even though occasionally I feel bad for disrupting.

Hadir knows a secret way into Kabul Stadium. He believes practicing soccer on that field will one day make him a star, just like Nikpai. Some weeks there's a night guard, but none ever keep the job for long. Nobody wants to go near, nobody but Hadir. At first, I tell him it isn't right. That it's strange wanting to be so close to the dead. But he calls me sissy, which he knows I hate even more than juggling the ball by myself, so I go with him. There isn't actually anybody buried there, but so many Afghans were tortured inside the stadium, everyone knows it's haunted.

At night, Hadir dribbles the ball down the alley between apartments and tosses pebbles onto the roof where my family sometimes sleeps. Once, a pebble hit my baby sister, and she had a fit, keeping my mother awake the rest of the night. "Hurry up, Pirooz!" Hadir will shout, "Let's go!" And I'll dash away, ignoring mother. My father works at night for the local police. Sometimes all he does is sit in a cement block building with other officers. Hadir is an orphan. We do as we please.

Inside the stadium, row after row of bleachers form a bowl around bright green grass that glows, even in the dark. There's nothing else in Kabul this color, "the color of prosperity," our newspaper called it. They didn't mention how so much blood leeched into the soil, the top foot was dug up and replaced before officials got anything to grow. Hadir and I play barefooted, kicking up soil and clumps of grass. We make long passes with the ball, panting up and down the sidelines to train both legs for well-aimed kicks. "Faster, Pirooz, faster," Hadir calls, and together we get lost in the work of it.

Our teacher used to wear a burqa, but now she doesn't. I study her lips when she speaks, two plump dates that open and close in this way I can't forget. I've never seen skin that looks so soft. Like you could press her lips with your fingertips and they would sink, as if into a pillow. I watch her silently and wonder. The Taliban executed teachers like her. Or sometimes, the Taliban amputated their hands. When our teacher moves up and down the aisles of the classroom, she runs her hands along the edge of each desk. I hold my breath when she comes near, imagining her wrists as puffy stumps, no hands or fingers with which to write.

Everybody knows the Taliban used to hang body parts from the stadium goal posts as an example. I never went to see the torture, but men in my neighborhood did. "Allahu Akbar!" they would shout when they returned home from the frenzy. I heard them talking, the bloodshed they described. They fired AK47's and danced in the streets, sometimes chattering for hours as the families on my block tried to sleep. I was tiny, four or five, but their tone made an impression on me; men's voices echoing through the alleys, a wretched, powerful kind of laughter that I understood had nothing to do with comedy.

Hadir often asks me to play goalie during our secret practices in Kabul Stadium. I stand in front of the repainted white goal posts that seem to float in the moonlight against the darkened stadium benches. He takes aim and kicks full strength, the leather ball slapping into my palms, against my chest, off my forehead. When I miss, I have to chase the ball to the outer edges of the field where I feel spooks trying to grab at me. Still, Hadir aims again and again, as though he can see a crowd roaring just for him all night long.

Later, we lie on our backs and look at the star-pocked sky. Hadir plucks fistfuls of grass from the field. Each clump radiates an infused, lime light from his palms, like he's holding an electric gem. Grass blades scratch at my back and tickle my nose.

"This must be what it smells like at the World Cup," Hadir says and tosses grass into the air.

"Maybe," I say. I think about the souls of Afghans trying to claw their way out of the ground. "Maybe not."

"By the time we're old enough, things will be different," he says.

"They already are."

"Not really, Pirooz, not like our teacher promises."

"Well, what do you mean?" I wonder if he's thinking about his parents, whatever his life was like before.

"I mean, there could be people celebrating and people forgetting to be afraid," he says. "Like all the infighting just disappearing so the rest of us can live our lives. There could even be soccer teams, coaches."

"Sounds good to me," I say. Hadir tosses the ball straight into the air a few times, catching it just above his nose. The wind blows and sweat cools on my skin.

"I came here once before the war," he finally says. "The Taliban were rounding people up. I got swept into the crowd. A man picked me up and carried me into the stadium. There were other kids in there too, waving their hands. We filled all the rows in that first section." He sweeps his arms in a circle around the stadium, indicating several thousand close-range seats.

"Hadir?" I say.

"They tortured women on the soccer field for adultery that day."

"Hadir, I don't want to know."

"But there's no way to tell if the women really did anything wrong."

"I remember," I say. I hated the trials the Taliban used to hold. They made it a game with rules that changed for convenience.

"I can still see them sometimes," he says, and the way he carries on, I can see them, too. Half a dozen mothers buried up to their waists in the penalty box, helpless against the stoning, their blood-stained burqas flapping in the wind like wings that could never quite lift them to safety.

We walk home slowly that night, passing the ball in short punts across the narrow streets. Hadir likes to aim for the base of streetlights, aligning the ball so it will bounce my direction and set me up for the next, easy pass. A few stray dogs linger behind, limping and skinny. They'd probably eat Hadir's soccer ball if we left it. Nights like this, I can almost forget our dim-lit city was the center of a warzone. The fighting moved north, so everyone calls this the good time. Some men linger outside their homes. Beggars sleep restlessly in old cars, under shop awnings. Mostly, though, people rest at this hour.

During recess the next day, Hadir and I show the other students our grass-stained feet. They cluster around, marveling at the color, bright green streaks against dusty, brown toes. One boy, Waafiq, doesn't believe our adventures.

"That's not from grass." He points. "You found your mother's makeup."

But as soon as he says it the other boys laugh and point at him. "How would you know?" they jeer.

Waafiq shushes and sulks unsteadily toward the schoolhouse.

"Wait. Come back this way."

"If you're going to poke, I'm not coming," Waafiq says. He's younger, maybe nine. He limps when he walks, because there's a piece of shrapnel in his calf the size of a cashew. Everybody knows.

"I won't poke. I have an idea," I tell him. "We need you."

Hadir shoulders into the center of the circle, catching on. "That's right," he says. "We need everybody to play."

For the next two weeks we train double-time, and it feels even more difficult to study. Our teacher paces the aisles during arithmetic. She paces during religious studies. She seems only to stand still for geography quizzes, using a long stick to point at countries with tricky names. Each time she turns her back, we raise our leopard fists—all of us now—saluting Nikpai who came from nothing and turned it into pure bronze around his neck. Recess, Hadir teaches the other boys—young or spoiled, smart or slow—about defense and offense, hand-balls and throw-ins. He shares his soccer ball and has more friends than ever. "We're practicing for the Great Game," he tells them, and we scheme and plan, deciding on a date. By nighttime, we two hustle to Kabul Stadium, the city blocks our warm-up drill. The second our heels sink into that soft, radiant field, we're hearts-pounding, muscles-working ready to play. We walk home so tired, even the strays trot past, tails between their mangy legs. Hadir and I are always equals until we get to my block. Then I disappear into my family's apartment, and he turns down the alley, shadow moving like a ghost along the sidewalls. He says he lives close, but that's all. I never ask further.

The afternoon before the Great Game, our geography lesson is interrupted by an air raid. Sirens wail across the city like crying mothers. There's no basement, no bunker. Our teacher lines us against the wall. "Sit," she says. "Stay quiet." I stare at the maps and imagine myself further and further away: *Tajikstan, Uzbekistan, Turkemenistan.* Between sirens, I brace for a bone-shattering blast that never comes. *Azerbaijan, Armenia, Georgia.* More sirens, my muscles woven as tightly as a rug. *Turkey, Romania, Austria.* I go so far I can't even see war—*Germany, Scotland*—all the way to the North Atlantic Ocean. Then silence. Next, two footsteps. Three. Four. We are twenty-two boys in a room, forty-four feet that can run, one gigantic breath being held. I study our teacher's face, but she seems lost, prayers spilling from her mouth like broken teeth.

The schoolmaster appears, face dotted with sweat. "There's one hour before the next raid," he says. "We move now, or we're stranded overnight." Our teacher nods, and we follow her quickly through the hallways. She helps the smallest children first, lifting them into the schoolmaster's truck parked alongside our schoolhouse.

"You and Hadir are oldest," she says to me. "Take the rest to their houses. Don't stop along the way." She slides into the passenger seat and they disappear down the dusty road.

Hadir carries Waafiq on his back, taking alley shortcuts to our neighborhood. I shove and shuffle the others behind him. A few start to cry. "Where do you live?" I demand. I have to slap some to help them speak. Most are siblings and live together. When I get to my own home, I pound and pound until my mother unhooks the latch. Already, she's gathered my sisters, a satchel of food, and two jugs of water, sheltering them in our back room with a pile of mattresses. Together, we wait for sundown, knowing things could very suddenly grow worse.

No school for three days. Everything quiets. My city must look like a sleeping giant, all its window-eyes sealed shut. Families on my block know exactly what to do, sharing supplies and whispering favorite Afghan folktales to soothe the children at night. They tell the story of Buzaak Chinie, the Porcelain Goat. Or my old favorite, The Silver on the Hearth, where the poor farmer is rewarded with snakes that turn into coins. But I'm older this time and see the adults gossip. Something happened in Pakistan, they say, and now angry defectors from the Afghan National Army want to organize in Kabul. Or five Marines were shot south of the city and we hide in fear of retaliation. But another man says it wasn't Marines, it was an Afghan family, a mistake—a Red Cross station blown into a crater three meters deep. "But no bombs were dropped," I hear his brother argue. "It's all pretend to distract from the truth up north," another says. The radio confirms nothing, only repeats its static messages about precautionary measures. There are no errands. No boys playing santoors in the alley. No street vendors. No hot chai or kites. And of course, no Great Game.

When school reopens, this time everyone returns, no missing students. But our teacher wears her burqa again, a stone-blue curtain of fabric separating her from us. It's only her hands we can see now, and they appear more delicate than before.

"Hadir," I whisper. "What does it mean? Why does she hide?"

"Didn't you hear?" he says. "A doctor and three women were killed in Kunduz. He'd been helping female patients hide from their husbands."

"Who did the killing?" I ask.

"Who do you think?"

Our teacher is too hesitant to be outdoors, so the schoolmaster stays with us for recess that day.

"I still think she's foolish," Hadir says. "She shouldn't even be teaching. She should be at home. There's a reason women are safest at home."

"But aren't you grateful?" I ask. "At least we have someone to teach us."

Hadir glares at me. "Grateful? Easy for you to say." He dashes across the school grounds to teach the others more of his soccer smarts. I watch for a few moments as they dart back and forth, the smallest boys tripping over the ball, tumbling in the dust. I should help, but something in me turns sour and I tell the schoolmaster I'm ill, air settling in my throat like paste. He lets me go indoors to rest out of the sun.

Without any students inside, the classroom feels suspicious, as though this is how it will look if a giant bomb ever takes our city. The teacher sits at her desk, shoulders curled inward, hands trembling like they're holding a secret. I can hear the way she breathes, as quick and shallow as a shrew. Maybe Hadir was right.

Why do we bother with her arithmetic? Her silly lists of famous men? At the end of the day, the smartest boy in school can't undo his bloodlines, and no matter who our teacher is, Hadir will always be an orphan.

Our teacher shifts in her seat then lifts her head as if to look at me, eyes barely visible through the thick fabric. For a moment, I see how I easily could hurt her, how I could tear the burqa from her face as though every person in every country on that map could see her lies, those lips that promised us so much. But she is merely a grain of sand. She can never give her best like Nikpai. Not here, not now. My country won't let her.

Hadir doesn't come for me that night, so I find my way to Kabul Stadium without him. It's a full moon and the grass looks a pulsing, bright gray, as though the entire city has turned two colors—the color of night, and the color of moonlight reflecting off whatever it touches. I see Hadir sprinting downfield, cutting through the lighted grass and hear the gentle *thwap* of his bare foot against real leather. When he turns to run back downfield, he notices me and stops near the side goal posts, leaning forward to rest his hands on his knees and catch his breath.

After a minute, he shouts my direction: "We can't play on the same team."

"What do you mean?"

"Everyone from school got scared to play in the Great Game. You have to be the captain of one side and I'll be the captain of the other. That's all we've got. One-on-one."

"Okay," I say. "But no keeping score."

Hadir walks a few paces until he's standing in the exact center of the goal. He squats slowly, gaze upturned, then leaps to catch the cross post with both hands. He dangles easily, feet swaying, one side of his body outlined by the angling moonlight.

"This is what they looked like," he says and drops one hand so that his body hangs crooked, the other hand still wrapped around the post. "Except no body. Just an arm. Hanging there like it was a flag or something. And they never hung just one thing. There were always more..." He studies his own arm as though apart from himself.

"Hadir?" I say and walk toward him. "I'm sorry about today at school."

He returns his other hand to the post and swings his body until he gains enough momentum to swivel up top. "It's okay," he says finally. "You should really see it from up here. It makes the field look like it stretches forever."

I shimmy up the side of the goal post, teetering at the top. Hadir scoots my direction and offers his shoulder for balance. Once situated, we slide sideways toward the center of the goal, legs dangling beneath us.

"Wow," I say and look out at the field. "You're right." It extends perfectly straight, yard after endless yard, cleaner and brighter than anything in all of Kabul.

"How many people do you think will come to celebrate Nikpai?" Hadir asks.

"Our teacher said four thousand can fit," I say. "But I think even more will come."

"I think so, too."

We sit silently for some time, as the moon appears to move further away in the sky.

"You know what's funny?" I ask.

"What?"

"I think this is the most peaceful spot in Afghanistan."

Hadir laughs. "Yeah, maybe."

Just then, an odd hissing sound erupts around us, quiet at first but louder with each second. My breath catches, heart pounding in my throat. Hadir and I glance at each other, then look down the ever-reaching field to see a symmetrical array of sprinklers raised in the moonlight, reflective umbrellas of water spraying from each head.

"One," I say.

"Two," he says.

"Three!" we shout together and leap from the goal post to land triumphantly next to the soccer ball. Just like that, Hadir runs and dribbles. I sprint down the opposite sideline, leaping over sprinkler heads, laughing at the mess of it all. He kicks a long pass and I push harder, feet pumping against the saturated soil, trying to beat the ball to the sideline. The leather slaps the inside of my foot. Trap. Go. Hadir darts downfield, shouting "Here, Pirooz! Here!" His feet slice through shimmering grass, and he's almost to the penalty box, when I think of Nikpai, the way nobody thought an Afghan could win an Olympic medal. I make the final pass and fall onto my back, sprinklers showering me with water. When I hear Hadir grunt to take his shot on goal, I don't have to look to see if he's made it. I raise my leopard fist and shout at the sky. Somewhere in the distance, Hadir hollers back, the ghosts of Kabul Stadium hollering right along with him.

JUST THE DOG AND ME

I'm outside in the middle of the night again, just the dog and me. The whole neighborhood's asleep. Cooper's sniffing every blade of grass, checking the perimeter of the yard. Just the kind of thing that drives Marcia nuts. But I can be patient. I can be patient with his mini mission to protect and defend, because the longer I watch him the more I understand his logic.

He's all tail and nose, tugging the leash this way and that, sending muted snorts into the night—a canine Morse code. Any minute now, the neighbor's Beagle will probably hear us. Set the whole block singing. Cooper freezes for a moment, the leash tight between us, then before I know it he's sending up more dirt than a landmine, and I just drop the leash and let him dig.

It's a beautiful thing, going after what you want like that.

Some nights, I see shooting stars by the dozen out here. They streak across the sky like tracer fire, faster than you can say, "Incoming!" Tonight though, the moon's a smile, and when Cooper lifts his muzzle from the hole to see if I'm still here, watching his back, I can barely make out his shape through the dark.

I hear the click of the front door, and Marcia steps outside.

"Patrick, is that you again?" she whispers. "Are you out there?"

I don't say a thing. But I can sense Cooper as he turns with me toward the door. He takes point, and we move silently through the grass. Marcia doesn't hear us until we're close enough for me to put my arm around her waist and say, "Right here, baby. I'm right here."

She yelps, and does a little half-hop across the porch. "Cooper's licking my toes," she says. "He's tickling me." Then she laughs, and it must be the easiest sound I've ever heard. It doesn't take much before the neighbor's dog starts yowling, which only makes Marcia laugh louder and I'm thinking, *Yeah. That's it. We're all out here just trying to get somebody to listen, aren't we?*

AMPUTEE

Today is my 112th day at Walter Reed. After two more weeks of physical therapy and some fittings, I might be ready to leave. That's the way the doctors keep saying it, "Just a few more weeks, Becca." They're in a fuss about scar tissue and nerve endings, not to mention the shrapnel wounds. Compared to most soldiers here, I'm a cakewalk case. But from my perspective, I've never felt more high maintenance in my life.

I'm in here for my arm. Half of my arm, really. That's the way I think on a good day. Other days, I think like this: I left one elbow joint, 28 bones, twice as many muscles and tendons, one wrist, and my entire left hand in the middle of a filleted Humvee on the outskirts of Karbala, Iraq. I never heard the bomb detonate. There was me, thrown twenty feet from the vehicle, and there was my arm, tangled into the steering wheel and engulfed in flames faster than you can say, "Don't look."

Yesterday, I walked through the hospital gardens before lunchtime. The only part of me that felt alive was the part that wasn't there at all. I could sense the wind move inside of me when I walked, like the air got trapped in the ghost-hollow of my forearm. It whirred around in there, tickling my mind. I couldn't believe the sensation. I sat down on one of the benches and waited until no one was looking. Finally, I reached my good arm across my body and groped for my missing arm. I thought maybe I'd catch a flare of feeling across my palm and be able to remember, but when I grabbed, nothing came back to me.

I tried to get up and go back inside but my legs felt like sandbags. I stared at my good arm and then at the greenery. All around, tall day lilies and goldenrod waved their petaled hands in the breeze. The garden flashed between sun splotches, pinpricked and day-glow like the outlines of base camp during a pelting, red sandstorm.

My buddy PFC Gunther must have seen me in the garden, because next thing I knew, he took the elevator down and wheeled himself over to the bench. He has his arms, but both legs are in the freezer. That's what he tells people who are nosy.

"I'll trade ya' injuries," he said.

I looked at him slowly. I knew he wanted me to say what I always said, but my lips felt pasted closed. I forced a smile, then gave him my line: "You don't want to lose your beer-drinking hand, do you?"

He smiled, then turned serious. "What're you doin' out here, anyway?"

"Nothing."

"Fastest way to get into trouble," Gunther said. Gravel crunched beneath the wheels of his chair as he rolled back and forth.

"Faster than a jihadi can turn a tank round into an IED?" I asked.

"Yup," he said. When he chuckled, it sounded like the quiet rumbling of tanks in the distance. "C'mon." He wheeled back to the main entrance and I followed him toward the cafeteria.

"Race you down the hall for some chow!" I said and took off at a slow jog.

"Hey, now, Specialist," he hollered. "Man's greatest invention was the wheel and I've got two of 'em." He dodged a few nurses and cut me off. When I ran, half of me felt like lead, the other half like air. I hated how my left side lurched forward so much quicker than my right. My stump throbbed like a second heart, blood pooling around the fleshy scar tissue, trying to go where it could not.

In the cafeteria, they put the food trays on the tables ahead of time, all portioned out. It's just easier that way. I sat down near one of the windows, and Gunther went off to the bathroom. He was good at that now, he liked to remind everyone, always shouting a triumphant "Yeehaw!" from the stalls when he'd successfully lifted himself from chair to commode. I stared at the beige food tray in front of me: one hamburger, coleslaw, condiment cups, and a bag of Fritos. Just like that, my world shrank to about two feet—the distance between where my left arm used to be and where that impossible bag of chips lay, sealed closed.

Everybody wants to know the first thing I'd do if I had my arm again. They always think of the easy stuff, like hug my kid or shoot a basketball. I just want to hurt somebody back, even though it isn't right. I know exactly what I'd do, transported to Karbala with my body whole again, a bearded Iraqi man cowering at my feet. He'd plead for his life, and I'd raise my left arm, curling my palm around his throat until he withered into ten thousand grains of sand. Can't you see it? The way this war has made us both a mess?

I don't know how long I sat there staring at that tray of food, but when Gunther came out of the bathroom and found me at the table, he sounded like he was talking under water. The bag of chips lay crushed beneath my shoes.

"Specialist?" he said. "Hey. *Becca?*"

"Yeah. What?"

"Becca, your family's here. Look." Gunther nodded toward the cafeteria entrance.

I stood slowly, chips scraping underfoot. My little girl ran up and grabbed my right hand, swinging our arms back and forth like the simplest thing in the world.

"Easy now," I told her, but she just kept on swinging, her hand folded softly into mine, all that sweetness pressing into me through her perfect, little palm.

PERMANENT WAVE

Daniel plays the scene over again in his mind. The first moments come easily—forty-seven thousand fans pushing up from their seats, arms lifting overhead at just the right moment to create a sensational, stadium-wide wave. He'd been invited to throw the first pitch of the Seattle Mariners' season, Michael Pineda walking with him to the mound almost like buddies, almost like he and Daniel had been signed the same year or might talk stats in the locker room after the game. Almost.

Just like how Daniel feels about this whole business of being a hero, of being asked to kick off the season because he lost his right arm in Iraq. It all seems almost right: he almost died but didn't, the doctors almost saved his right arm but couldn't, his thoughts during recovery almost turned suicidal but—well, here he stands. Back in the real world: almost normal looking if the angle is right, almost used to the ghost-limb-sensation, almost sleeping through the night without frantic flashbacks.

After "The Star Spangled Banner" (Daniel lifting his left hand to his heart, an awkward honoring of the flag that took so much of him), Pineda winked, then gently tossed him the ball. Did anyone else notice? Somewhere between the ball leaving Pineda's fingertips and settling into Daniel's left hand, Daniel realized Pineda went easy on him. A sympathetic toss—nothing manly or pro-league about it—as though Daniel were a toddler and lacked the steadiness it took to complete the simple catch.

He likes to make the memory stop before that pass. It's better to focus on the beginning, all those fans on their feet just for him. They rise and fall from their seats as enthusiasm makes its way round and round the stadium. Forty-seven thousand fans in a permanent wave, all of them shaking, cheering, waving their arms so frantically it's like they'd give them up just to make Daniel feel whole again.

THAT SUNDAY MORNING
FEELING

I'm out back splitting wood again. It keeps my body busy while my mind's in a fray. The view from here captures the jagged line of the Sawtooth Mountains, Idaho's finest and just the kind of living I envision heaven to be. Wild. Quiet. A no-catch set up that has everything it needs. This time of year, the songbirds keep me company all day, readying for winter. I like the little buggers. They can tough it out up here even at 4,000 feet. Hollow bones! Can you imagine?

If I blur my vision, the peaks around me soften just enough to look like the L4 grid in northern Afghanistan, where I spent my third tour. First Kuwait, then Iraq, then Afghanistan. This last time, I led patrols for eight months from a forward operating base overlooking a narrow valley in the Hindu Kush. That gridline—the L4—mattered the most. Dip down into the valley toward the L5 and you'd run into what brought us there in the first place.

The woodpile looks pretty good this season, four cords of pine stacked neatly against the shed. I've been out here long enough for the day to warm up, so I peel off my sweater and sit down on the chopping block for a breather. I can hear Helen humming in her studio at the main house, ten meters through the woods. She does this painting thing, landscapes and inspirationals. Between my pension and her business, it's enough. And when I can muster the patience to fill out forms, a few months later we get a reimbursal check from the military for my head juice. That's what I call the therapy and even though it costs five times what it should and seems more about being nosy than helping somebody out, I go anyway. My promise to Helen. One hour, twice a week. The least I can do after all the anniversaries and holidays I missed.

I've been back four months and still feel crooked. Yesterday, the therapist asked me what I think is missing since my return from Afghanistan.

"I miss my Sunday mornings," I told her.

"Do you attend services?"

"No," I said. "Not that kind of thing. What I mean is, I miss that feeling. Like all your work is done, and there's still a whole, bright day ahead of you."

"Say more," she said. But I couldn't.

She pulled out the 2900, this new post-deployment form all the guys are filling out. It's for health problems that don't show up until getting back home. First off, she needed a point of contact—somebody who could reach me at all times, no matter what. I gave her Helen's cell, but I wanted to tell her I couldn't even reach myself half the time.

The part of the form about chemical weapons exposure, ionizing radiation, depleted uranium—all that seemed easy. I just didn't see much of it, if any. But then she asked: Human blood or body parts? Smoke from burning feces or oil fires? Were there any sudden or unanticipated loud noises?

"Hold on, hold on," I said.

She put her pen down and set the form aside.

"It's not the fact of experiencing those things," I said. "We all saw that kind of stuff. But here's the deal: when I was in the middle of it all, it didn't affect me. I didn't feel a thing."

Later, I told Helen about the session. She finished a painting that day and wanted me to see it. It depicted our woodpile, baking in the afternoon light. At the end of the pile, she painted my ax with a tiny junco perched on the tip of the handle. I told her the wood looked so real, somebody could get a splinter just by touching the canvas.

If I could be anything else in the world, I think I'd be one of those songbirds. I wouldn't have to leave the Sawtooths, or even Helen, really. I'd still keep an eye on things, just from a different vantage point. As for what's missing—that Sunday morning feeling—I'd have it back again, tucked inside my bones like a weightless, secret weapon providing strength, even through the toughest winter.

GETTING PERSPECTIVE

I packed up all his things. They're where they need to be. I don't go smelling pillowcases or lying in bed for days, and I don't expect pity. There's a support group that meets at Blue Ridge Hospital, twenty mountain-miles into town. I go once a week even if I'm grumpy. The plastic chairs squeak, and the conference room is always cold, but going there feels more like a Carolina God-throb than anything I ever had in some building with a steeple. What I mean is, it feels all right, so I keep going back.

Buns went to Iraq, but I don't ever say that out loud: one, because it sounds like he left me for bullets, two, because he made me promise never to tell anyone I called him that, and three, because it sounds like something with a bad ending. You should know from me saying that, Buns never came home. He died in that racket of a war, and you should also know just because this sounds trite doesn't mean it can't be true: He was the only man I ever loved. He knew me better than my own skin. There's no replacing that.

Buns was Ben. Benjamin Colton Young, one of too many Youngs to count in the Blue Ridge Mountains but the only one I couldn't stop looking at. Ben's mom says good looks hid for five generations of Youngs, then came out all at once on him. Like the rhodies blooming atop Roan Mountain in summer, everything polished and glowing from the inside out. It might not make

sense, comparing him to a mountain, but now that he's gone I feel
him around me even stronger, lodged into the horizon. Ben's mom
also says I'm going to have to relearn myself, but all I have to say to
that is, there's no time. *Single mom.* Two words I thought I'd never
put next to each other, but now I'm one of them, which is a heck
of a lot better than a spider that kills. Widow? I've had enough of
death. The last thing I need is people calling me something I'm
not.

Ben homeschooled, then started junior year at Mitchell High
the same year I graduated. He worked after school bagging
groceries at Hughes Market where it was my job to unlock the
tobacco case anytime somebody wanted a pack of Camels. That
year, Ben's kid brother overdosed on crystal, and he missed a week
of pay. The paper ran the story. Everyone in town said Patrick
convulsed for hours in the ER, rattling the hospital bed like the
rapture.

Sometimes, I gave Ben a ride home after work. He got to
Hughes Market on the school bus but couldn't always thumb a
ride out of the valley after close. His family's trailer squatted at the
base of Pinch Ridge on cinderblock piers—a Carolina Country
doublewide the color of spent Levi's and just about as worn. I lived
with my folks further up the holler in a stone-faced house with a
white porch and tin roof.

Our first date, we hiked Pinch Ridge to the apex and climbed
the radio tower at dusk. Two hours uphill and another half mile
along, I led Ben to a mowed patch of mountaintop and heavy
fencing.

"Do you want to climb it?" I asked and nudged him a step
toward the guard fence.

"Have you done it before?"

"Once," I lied.

"Lillis, you're too much," he said, but I saw the corners of his mouth holding back that rhodie smile.

We both knew about climbing chain-link fences, but taking hold of that first rung of the maintenance ladder at about eye level was another matter. My heart dropped to my stomach. How could I have been so brave and so chicken-scratch at the same time? I looked up at the ladder, and Ben put his hands on my waist. I think about that moment a lot. How I could feel his focus, everything in him pulsing right through his palms and into me. I reached for the ladder, and before I knew it, the toes of my boots hooked over the first rung. I felt light and scared in the same breath, exactly the same way I'd feel a few years later right before our wedding vows. Now I know that feeling means something good's going to happen next, even if it ends differently down the line.

About two-thirds of the way up, Ben hollered to stop. He climbed a few more rungs and put us face-to-face, our bodies pressed so tight into the ladder I could feel his stomach arching into mine. We breathed together and there was nowhere to look but straight into him.

"You okay?" he asked, barely a whisper.

"Yeah, I'm okay." My heart skipped around like a squirrel across hardtop. Our fingers wrapped end-to-end around the sides of the ladder, knotted fists as tight as rope.

"We don't have to go all the way to the top," Ben said.

We leaned into each other and I felt the ladder dig into my ribcage. The world up there smelled like ice. Fresh and piercing. Ben loosened his grip and stretched his arm across my back to the other side of the ladder, holding me steady. Then he kissed me like he meant it and part of me crawled inside of him and never looked back. That was our beginning. You know the ending. In between, we had ten years.

Hattie hired me after Buns died. Hers is the only late-night diner in the county, and she knows I need the money. I stopped homeschooling our two girls (Jenny's nine, Tina six) and put them in elementary that August, then signed up for the day shift. Mrs. Young comes to sit with the girls two nights a week so I can keep my evening classes at the college extension earning my certification as a high school math teacher.

A few weeks into my second semester, a new Ed major, Zachary, walked me to my car after class.

"What's your hurry, anyway?" Zachary asked. His sneakers scuffed along the sidewalk, loose concrete crunching as he walked.

"I've got things waiting for me at home." I pulled my keys from my bag. It felt true saying it. I'd always had things waiting for me at home. Now it was just different things.

"Can I take you out sometime?"

I shifted the bag to my other shoulder and unlocked the truck. Zachary didn't live in Mitchell County. He didn't know. I opened the truck door and shook my head. "I've got two kids," I told him. "And a job." A few students from class got into their cars nearby, another paced along the sidewalk, waiting for her ride.

"Your kids can come," he said. "I was thinking about The Pizza Stop in Avery. I know it's far but my cousin owns it. The calzone sauce is our family recipe."

After Buns died, I'd debated about wearing my wedding ring, but people in support group offered mixed feelings. Eventually, I wrapped the ring in a scrap of velvet and stored it between the mattresses in our bedroom.

"Some day when we don't have class, maybe?" Zachary said. "It'd be my treat."

"Sorry," I told him, and when I turned to say *See ya*, I nearly bumped into his chest. He held his arm on the upper edge of the doorframe, propping himself as he leaned toward the truck. His body and the driver's side door formed a tent around me. I hadn't smelled a man up close in months, and he didn't smell right. Not bad, but not right. I slid onto the seat and Zachary stepped away. I closed the door, then rolled the window down. "Gotta run," I told him. "Single mom."

Sunday is family day. Most people are already tucked away in pews while Jenny and Tina and me hop into the truck and try to find whichever mountain peak they can point to along the horizon. I tell them as long as we can make it to Grandma Young's house in time for Sunday dinner, I'll take them wherever they want to go. Their favorite is a spot over in McDowell called Buck Mountain. There's a fire tower there, and last Sunday, Tina finally built the nerve to climb it. Must have thought about it eight or ten times before that, always sniffling a little when her braver sister hustled up the plank steps without her. I held Tina's hand the whole way up, and when we reached the top I forgot everything for a moment, breathless with the crisp, fall-colored view.

After Sunday dinner, I stood on the porch steps with Mrs. Young. The girls sat inside watching TV with their grandpa. Mrs. Young told me when her Ben was Jenny's age, it wasn't heights but depths that gave him the spooks. They have a natural pond behind their trailer, and Ben and Patrick played there most summer afternoons with their cousins. One day, Ben's older cousins dunked him so many times he sucked down a mouthful of water and came up coughing until he vomited.

"Didn't do anything but wade after that," Mrs. Young said. We looked out at the pond. Dense, green grasses and blackberry brambles rimmed the edge, so thick deer could hardly find their way for a drink. Crickets hollered into the growing dusk. "That pond makes my backyard smell like a sweet, rotting pie!" Mrs. Young laughed. "Poke around long enough, and you'll come out berry-stained. Purple from calf to toes." She shook her head as if remembering something from centuries ago, rather than decades ago. Not even sixty and lost both sons.

Buns never wanted to be buried. His orders called for cremation after science finished with his body, which is why his one-year is marked on my calendar. It takes that long for the ashes to come back. It's been half that long now, and if I had a dollar for every time Mrs. Young tried to give me advice about moving on, I'd be rich enough to undo time. "Fake it till you make it," she tells me. What I want to tell her is, mothering isn't something you forget. But there's this other part of me—the ways I knew myself only by being around Buns—that feels like it's gone forever. How do you move on from something you can't even find anymore?

There's a place Buns took me on our honeymoon that even Mrs. Young doesn't know about. The night of our wedding, everyone thought we left for the coast. But I never made the reservations. Buns didn't want me to. He said he wanted to plan it for us and keep it a surprise. After our reception, we piled into the truck and headed south a little ways to the Smoky Mountains. He'd found a cabin in the Catalochee Valley, and it was all ours for four days.

Buns waited until dusk the next night to show me the real surprise. We drove to an open pasture a bit further down the road. There, in the hazy, purple light, a dozen elk gathered to graze. They'd been re-introduced a few months prior, but nobody I knew from Mitchell County had come to see them yet. They moved slowly through the grasses, like careful giants, and I marveled at their thick, dark fur—the way it blended perfectly with the dying light. Eventually, we got out of the truck and walked a few feet to the edge of the road. Buns wrapped a sleeping bag around my shoulders and stood behind me, held me tight.

We must have watched for hours, first studying their dense silhouettes from antler to withers to legs. As night fell, we sensed them by sound: grasses rustling then torn from the soil, followed by rhythmic, tooth-to-tooth chewing. Strange to think what those antlers could do, how those hooves could crush. But I knew Buns didn't show me the elk to scare me. Those elk made a new start together in the mountains. They had everything they needed in life to survive. If we played ours lives right together, we might, too.

A few weeks ago, Hattie asked me to sub on a Saturday night— ordinarily my time off. Her other head waitress couldn't make it, she explained, and with the monthly Rod & Gun Club reservation in the back room, she couldn't operate short-staffed. I arranged for the girls to sleep over with their grandparents and Hattie promised to let me work the back room, solo. "They'll be there all night," she warned me. "But they'll make it worthwhile." Eighteen of Mitchell County's finest, or so they described themselves, and I knew it was a chance to earn extra tips. I wanted to buy both the girls bicycles for Christmas. A night like this could make the difference.

It shouldn't have caught me off guard that Buns had known so many of the guys in Rod & Gun. It's a small county. But I hadn't so much as thought of his friends after Buns deployed.

"Lillis!" Taylor shouted. He'd been quarterback when Buns played kicker. Though he walked stiffer than an old man now, he still had that star-player build and trick-up-his-sleeves grin. "How you been?"

"Oh, you know," I said. "What can I get you to drink?"

"Those girls must be knee-high by now," he said. He had a wife once. She divorced him after six months.

"Taller than that," I said. "Keystone?"

Taylor nodded, and I worked my way around the table. There was Taylor's brother Christian who managed the mill, Wran who sold used tires from the lot next to Go-Mart, Lee that worked in real estate, and Robbie who fixed big rigs. Each dressed in their cleanest Duluth denims and button-ups; a few had slapped on aftershave and left their standard ball caps at home. From thirties to fifties, Buns had found a way to befriend all of them, though he never joined the club himself. By the time I reached the other side of the table, I felt shaky. It hit me then, how the room teemed with life. I'd been thinking about Buns for so many months but that was just in my mind. The back room felt wholly different than that, as if I'd put on a pair of 3-D glasses. The space buzzed and lifted, a hover of energy. Deep-voiced vibrations of laughter crisscrossed the air. I smelled boot polish, gunpowder, Old Spice, forest duff. My body bent toward all of it, but I felt confused. I found nothing to shape myself against.

When I got around to Joe Campbell, I knew what was coming.

"Joe!" I said, smiling. It's just what you do. "What'll it be?"

"Lillis, my God, you look half ghost," he said. Seven 'o clock and the guy was already toast. "You and Ben," he shook his head. "Jesus, what a mess."

"I wouldn't call it a mess," I said. The room quieted and a few men fiddled with their unused forks.

"That war's still on and you're not the only woman who's hurting without a husband these days. If that's not a mess, what would you call it?"

My heart slammed into my throat, and right there I could feel part of myself lift through the ceiling, out into the Appalachian sky. My eyes filled with water, but I pushed it back down. "Joe Campbell came out drunk," Buns had warned me once. "It's a wonder nobody's chopped off his tongue." I took a deep breath and drilled my eyes into Joe.

"What I would call it," I said, "is none of your goddamn business."

"Ah Lillis, lighten up, you know just as well as I do that—"

"Stop putting your foot in your mouth, Joe, and leave her be," Marshall said. He'd been Buns' best man at our wedding. "Come on down to this end of the table, Lillis. We've got manners and a few of us are thirsty." Several Rod & Gun Club members pounded the table using mock-Neanderthal gestures and the mood lifted enough for me to hustle my way through the rest of the orders.

When I got to Marshall, he spoke quietly at my hip. "Some things never change, Lillis. Don't mind him."

I looked at him and nodded, pen tip angling into my notepad. Marshall didn't make me ask for his order, just said it plain and simple and let me ease my way through the last few customers. I marked Joe down for the steak special, $12.95. Probably twice what he wanted to spend but, as far as I was concerned, that was hardly enough.

When I got home, the house felt doubly quiet with the girls gone. I drank a glass of wine, then got ready for bed. Under the covers, I rolled to Buns' side and curled into the dip from his body, making myself small inside the place he used to be. *Half ghost.* The words stabbed. I knew enough not to want something I couldn't have anymore, but I hated missing Buns the way I did. Full body, every cell. Joe Campbell could rot in the bottom of a pond as far as I was concerned, even if he was right. I wasn't only a half ghost; I was a widow. Death felt close enough to me to be my own name. I inched my body further beneath the covers, pressing my face into the sheets. When I cried, I thought about my ring buried between the mattresses. How even though I'd taken it off, I hadn't so much as started leaving Buns behind. I knew from support group I should call somebody, but the idea of conversation exhausted me. Besides, if I could have called anybody that night, I would have called Mrs. Young.

As soon as the girls got home the next morning, I knew I wanted to take them up to Pinch Ridge.

"C'mon," I said. "Get changed. We're going on a hike."

The girls were too little to hike the way Buns and I did that first date, so I drove us up Sweetwater Lane until we got to the service road. I parked the truck at the gate and told the girls to get out.

"Where are we going?" Jenny asked.

"That radio tower up there," I said. "It's the spot your Daddy and I used to go together."

"Mama, I can't climb that," said Tina.

"Don't worry, sweetie. We're not going to. But there's something else I want you to see up there anyway."

"C'mon!" Jenny hollered. She worked her way between the bars on the gate and started walking along the ruts. Tina hustled after her.

The old road stretched about a mile and looked overgrown even that late into fall. Asters sagged from the weight of their heavy heads, purple blooms lining our way. The leaves were down, but the creepers still looked a bright, burnt red. They climbed the grey tree bark like arteries. Eventually, the forest thinned, and even the evergreens dropped off. It was open and grassy up top and wind pulled over the ridge like a riptide. I slipped my wool cap on and zipped my jacket, then jogged a little to catch up with the girls.

"Here," I said. "If we want to last at all, we'll need these." I passed them their winter hats. Jenny's was bright purple fleece with an embroidered flower Mrs. Young sewed last Christmas. Tina's was pink with a bobble on a string. It blew sideways in the wind like a little flag. "Almost there," I said. We walked slower, Jenny in one rut, Tina in the other. I walked the hump in between, their palms pressed into mine for warmth. The radio tower loomed a hundred yards away. Behind that, a granite outcropping cusped the perfect view. Buns and I used to take that road when we wanted to get up high, fast. "Nothing like a view to keep things in perspective," he would say. "Listen to you," I'd say. "Should have been a philosopher, not a soldier."

We got to the outcropping and I took it all in—the Black Mountains curving off the Blue Ridge, the Smokies in the near distance, miles more we couldn't even see. This world is vast. Our longing is just a speck on a mountaintop.

We could keep warm if we kept moving, so when the wind got under our skin, I decided to teach the girls how to make a cairn. I hefted the first few large rocks to set the base, then showed them what do next. Jenny added a rock about the size of her shoe. Tina topped it off with a fist-sized piece of granite, and together we stood back to examine our work. Barely a foot off the ground, but still, a mark had been made. I told them about Buns and me on our first date—not the climbing part—and let them know the outcropping on Pinch Ridge had been our special viewing place.

"It's yours now, too," I said. "So whenever you come up here, leave a stone for Daddy, okay?" They nodded and huddled in to me for warmth.

I took my time driving us home. The vents blasted hot air on our thighs and Tina nodded off. Down in the valley, Jenny and I saw something move along the highway.

"Huh!" Jenny gasped into a whisper when she saw it. "A fox!"

I slowed the truck, and we passed, the animal just twenty feet in the distance. It crouched low through the shrubs, then zipped along the fence. "Good eyes," I said. She smiled at me, face so much like her Daddy's I could almost see him on the other side of her.

"I love you, Jenny," I said.

"I know, Mama."

Three months later, the ashes arrived. I walked out to the garage to find the sourwood box that Buns's Grandpa Young made for us as a wedding gift. I opened the lid and started emptying the box. Buns kept one-of-a-kind fix-its in there: odd-sized washers, hooks I don't know the names for, even some antique brass knobs salvaged from an old dresser. I brought the box back into the house and dusted if off.

I can't tell you that pouring Buns's ashes into that box brought anything back to me. I can't even say whether I'll always keep them in there. But I can tell you my husband died in Iraq, and I'll say it out loud: one, because it's true, two, because he wouldn't want me keeping quiet about something that important, and three, because it sounds like the start of whatever happens next.

WIA

I felt a tiny itch in the back of my brain, like a dispatch from another world telling me to get up and get moving because something wasn't right. The sky? Downtown Bagdhad?

That's when Doc Triebold appeared, all sweat-faced and shouting. I watched his lips move but couldn't hear a thing. He grabbed the handle on the back of my flak vest and dragged me over rubble to the side of a building. I kept lifting my arm in a slow arc toward my stomach, only to have Doc swat it away. He looked at me and shouted again, but I couldn't even hear my own heartbeat. I felt it though, a platoon of frightened fists pounding inside my chest wall.

Then Connor appeared, tossing grenades, hollering "Frag out!" I read his lips, but more importantly I read his face, the way he turned away after glimpsing my midsection. I lifted my head to see but Doc moved quickly, slapping his palm across my forehead and pinning me to the sidewalk. The sky pulsed overhead like an electric blue ocean. My entire body felt backwards, as though I was falling up—not down—that fantastic sea-sky trying to suck me in.

Next thing I remember, bits of brick crumbled onto my face

and neck. Connor fired a few rounds, and I heard shell casings fall like coins to the sidewalk. Just like that, I had my ears back. My insides felt like a pit of quicksand, pain spiraling through my gut and out the other side. The gunfire quieted, then Doc and Connor hoisted me around the corner to a Humvee. I remember feeling guilty, like I should help them carry me out.

I made it to the field station and then onto a cargo plane filled with row after row of hanging cots. The members of my squad were long gone. Most, I'd never see again. Two men lifted me over their shoulders and set the rungs of my cot in line with a series of hooks. The cot above mine hung so close I could touch it. The outline of another soldier's body pressed through the canvas and his blood oozed through, dripping onto my legs.

I thought that was it, that we'd all die in that gigantic steel cave, cots swaying like bats as the plane's engine roared. But then a nurse came. And another. And another. IV bags, morphine drips, blood transfusions. The nurses darted like swallows from cot to cot, a silent, gentle army whose only mission was to keep us alive

MIA

Mazar-i-Sharif, 2002. Nothing pretty about it. Block by block, one structure at a time, our platoon and the rest of Bravo Company gutted the district for three days straight. Raw sewage ran in thick streams down the alleyways. Stray dogs roamed in packs, desperate for food. Once, I watched an old mutt nibble on a dead Afghan's wounds and nose into his flesh, rabid with hunger. The dog appeared embarrassed and lost, like a fallen dictator pillaging the remains of his own village.

It was my turn to provide security while one of our fire teams cleared a house. This corner had two soldiers on the street, myself guarding the doorway, and another two men on the roof opposite the building. I watched as my team charged into the house: First Smithfield with his boots, kicking that door right off its hinges, then taking a knee so he could cover for the others. Watson moved next, all 6'6" of him. He breezed over the threshold spraying an M16 from his hip, then cut left inside the doorway. Next up, Gunny Menendez: step, step, drop. He pivoted on one knee, aiming his weapon to the right. Last, I watched Nelson hustle straight through the entryway while the other team members provided cover. He came to the stairs at the left end of the hallway, his buddies now at his back, and led the charge up the steps. All four of them disappeared out of sight.

Outside, the sky clouded over, lending a muted haze of browns and grays to the city. I held my post, standing on the splintered front door. I looked left down the street—one white sedan and two scooters parked parallel with the sidewalk. To the right, a family of five hustled away from us. I looked left again. Right. Then up, across, and back down, tracing the line where the foundation of the building met the sidewalk. Other than looking, the biggest part of providing security was listening. The guys in 'Nam apparently warned, "If you hear the crickets stop, something's not right." In Mazar, there weren't any crickets, and the city birds had long since fled. But that day, I listened more for a feeling, a sort of crystal ball suspicion that something wasn't right.

Instead, I heard a single gunshot—not ours—then a breathless cry from Smithfield. "No!" he shouted. He bellowed from the second story. My body tensed in anticipation. Next up, the whole block shook, hunks of glass exploding from the windows.

I heard a thundering of footsteps and peered again down the hallway. A jihad fighter sprang down the stairs, Smithfield at his heels. The two zipped out the back door, and I sprinted after them. By the time I emerged into the back alley, the jihadi gripped Smithfield from behind, an M16 braced against his throat.

Our snipers hollered down and aimed their weapons. "We've got him, Smithfield. We've got him. Just hold steady." But the fighter shifted his weight and kept walking backwards, using Smithfield's wide frame as a body shield. None of us could get a clear shot. I stayed low and close along the alley wall, following them as they retreated for another block.

"Just shoot him through me," Smithy said. He started turning purple from the pressure of the gun against his carotid artery.

"It won't work," I hollered.

"Just shoot him. Shoot through my leg and into his," Smithy said, then he passed out. His body went limp, then rose slightly as the fighter twisted into a low crouch and started running, Smithy's body draped over his back like a gigantic rag doll.

"Call for backup," I shouted to our snipers. The jihadi lumbered through a narrow back door, crashing Smithy's limbs against the frame. Within seconds I reached the door and sprinted inside. Look left, right. Light filtered through a broken window, illuminating a looted living room, old blankets and cushions. I looked left again. Up. Across. Down. I'd never heard a silence as loud as the one filling that swollen moment, the moment my team leader Smithy completely vanished.

Backup arrived almost immediately, busting into the building from all directions. It didn't matter. Wherever that jihadi took Smithy, we weren't finding him. We dug up the entire district: every alley, building, doorway, closet, and mouse hole. Four blocks south of the initial firefight, I found Smithfield's Kevlar in the middle of the sidewalk. I remember hoping for a trick. Like if I touched the helmet Smithy'd surface through the concrete with that square-jawed, smart-ass smile of his, back in the game. But when I bent to pick it up, there wasn't an ounce of life left in it.

I radioed the location to our platoon sergeant, but back at headquarters they were already filling out paperwork. Missing in action. Last seen? As a hostage. Estimated location? Some place so horrific, even if I had a crystal ball I couldn't bring myself to look.

KIA

Camp Taji, Iraq, bunkroom 8B. Inventory of personal belongings, Specialist Donald R. Swaringon, Battle Roster #SW4982:

Walls

1 Seattle Mariners calendar. 2 postcards from "Sunny Hawai'i." 4 Christmas cards. 9 birthday cards. Approximately 17 photographs. 1 wooden cross. 1 small, pink teddy bear. 3 illegible children's drawings in crayon. 1 Post-It Note with the impression of a woman's lips in red lipstick. 1 Slim-Jim beef jerky wrapper tacked to the wall (presumably for sniffing). 1 door-sized pinup of J-Lo (likely also for sniffing). 1 miniature American flag.

Supply shelf

1 tube Blistex lip balm. 3 tubes Asics chafe-free sports performance gel. 5-pack Bic disposable razors, unopened. 8 packages baby wipes. 1 issue each of *Rolling Stone*, *Hustler*, and *Juggs*. 1 pack Clearasil face wipes.

Closet

6 cotton undershirts, 1 pair Nike running shoes, 6 pairs Under Armor athletic socks, 2 pair Army-issued black running shorts. 1 pair women's striped panties with the words "Love You!" scrawled

across the front. 1 Eastern Washington University sweatshirt. 1 flat of Peanut M&M's. 4 tubes Pringles. 2 packages Chips Ahoy. 1 half-eaten bag Doritos Cool Ranch.

Bookshelf:

Lord of the Rings by J. R. R. Tolkein. *Baseball Trivia*, Volume 3. *War and Peace* by Leo Tolstoy. Canon digital camera. Care package sent from Seattle dated 08 MAR 2010; stuffed with Kudos snack bars, Hanes briefs, small jar of stones labeled "Puget Sound," and 1 prepaid phone card. *There's Something About Mary, Charlie's Angels,* and *Being John Malkovich* DVD's (starring Cameron Diaz).

Duffel bag:

1 stone-carved elephant, 4 wooden bowls, and 1 hand-woven rug, each individually wrapped and labeled: Dad, Mom, Tiffany. Two children's T-shirts. (One for Justin, the newborn he hadn't met yet, and one for Sarah, the little blonde who sings in the bathtub and practices her step-ball-change on the coffee table.)

Inside pillow case:

King James Bible. Sealed envelope addressed to "Tiffany Swaringon, a.k.a. My bodacious babe." (It's what he called his wife when they were fooling around. They'd go back and forth like that. My slapstick sailor. My hell's bell's bride. My hubba-hubba husband. My maiden of mayhem. My too-hot, don't-stop, can't-live-without-you kind of man.)

THE GHOST OF SANCHEZ

I'm seven months into my eleven-month tour at Kunduz Military Base. Most of the stains on my uniform came from the blood of fellow soldiers, guys who got potted crouching right next to me. Here I am, untouched, no explanation. Lately, my mind feels like it's rigged with tripwire, a messy combo of the dumbest and most profound emotions I've ever experienced. Get a whole platoon of guys thinking like that, and no wonder we're trying to survive just as hard as we're trying to be the one who takes a hit and saves the next guy. It's almost like the movies, but I'm still here, my friends aren't coming back, and the blood leaking out of the hole in that haji's head isn't a Hollywood trick. Last month, I had to leave my buddy Sanchez's body in our tin-can-of-a-Humvee after the bridge we were trying to cross exploded. He was twenty-eight years old.

Our vehicle was first in the convoy that day—the worst place to be, though Sanchez never sweated it. The IED went off, and my stomach lurched when the bridge turned to powder beneath us. Three bullets spiraled into Sanchez's throat like a drill bit through sheetrock. He looked right at me—a slow motion, unforgettable gaze—then we dropped into the Kunduz, water over our heads in no time. I tried to push Sanchez out the window, but his body went limp, and everything turned red. I gave him one last shove, then swam toward the surface. Up top, water dripped from my helmet down my face, the salty taste of Sanchez's blood leeching into my mouth.

It took eight hours before a hero mission could finally retrieve the body. Sanchez wasn't coming up, and there wasn't any hope hooking our Humvee to a towline from the rockslide banks of the Kunduz. Finally, somebody called in a bridge crew to set up a temporary crossing. A team of Marines rappelled off the sides and combed through the riverbed until they found our rig. Then they found Sanchez.

I wasn't there for the extraction, but once they got him cleaned up enough, LT sent me to the morgue. Sanchez's throat had been ripped open, his face so bloated the mortician insisted on two visual confirmations before filing the final paperwork: PFC Ernesto Sanchez: cause of death, gunshot wounds to the throat and secondary drowning.

"It doesn't look like him," I told the mortician.

He peered over the top of his clipboard. "Specialist Dobson?"

"He's Mexican. He's darker than that. His skin isn't right," I said. I kept staring at Sanchez's left hand, the way his fingers still curled as if clutching the steering wheel. His flesh looked like the inside of a clam shell.

"Do you mean to tell me this isn't the body of Ernesto Sanchez?"

I stepped back from the table. I hadn't noticed until that moment, but the room looked unfathomably clean, walls wrapping me in a fluorescent whiteness as if to prepare my body next.

"Specialist Robert Dobson?"

"It's him," I said. "That's Sanchez."

I turned to leave, and that's when he found me—the ghost of Sanchez lifting right off the table, following me out of the morgue and across the base as I headed toward the bunkhouse. I knew right away no one else could see him, but sure as daylight, Sanchez was at my back. I kicked up a slow jog and Sanchez did too. The air felt dusty and dry, that same blasting sun beating down on me, illuminating Sanchez like a carp, reflective and wavering.

"What are you doing, man? What do you want?" I asked. I thought he might feel angry that I left him in the river, but Sanchez didn't make a sound. He gazed across the valley in the direction of the Hindu Kush Mountains.

I ducked into the bunkhouse and Sanchez followed. I had an hour before chowtime and needed to calm my nerves. I slouched in front of the PlayStation for a round of NBA Shoot Out. Somebody had left a Taco Bell wrapper on the floor, rancid Chalupas stinking like sewage.

"I suppose this is what the recruitment packet meant by 'creature comforts,'" I said and kicked the bag into the corner. "The same old shit you just don't need." Sanchez nodded, smiling a little to himself. Before he died, whenever he saw a soldier in line outside the PX for fast food, he'd try to come up with the foulest description possible. "*Yo quiero* heart surgery," he said once. Our commanding officer stood within earshot, a half-eaten Gordita in his meaty palm.

I waved the PlayStation control at Sanchez. "Do you want to play a round?" He shrugged and settled onto his bunk, leaving no impression in the mattress. I putzed around on the court for a few minutes, fake crowd roaring as if I'd taken my home state to the championships. Then out of nowhere, Sanchez bolted upright and brought his hand to his throat, slowly running his fingertips along the side of his neck and looking at me.

"That's right, man. That's where it happened," I said and

patted my own neck to confirm. "The bridge was rigged. We were ambushed."

He nodded in way that let me know he remembered.

"I don't know what else to say, Sanchez, and I sure as hell don't know what you're still doing here." I shook my head and said the next part real easy. "Like this, I mean. Like a ghost."

Admitting it made me blush. I didn't believe in ghosts. Who did?

Two days later, the company commander organized a memorial service and asked if I'd prepare the battlefield cross. Sanchez helped. By this time, I didn't mind. It never occurred to me that his presence was unnatural in this land of death and dirt and no-holds-barred. Besides, I felt certain his ghost would leave me after everyone paid respects.

We walked to the air hangar together, and I borrowed a three-step set of transportable stairs used for boarding smaller planes. The stairs belonged to the Germans, who also operated from our base. We used these for the foundation of any battlefield cross. I could have borrowed some from an American plane, but Sanchez always fantasized about Europe, his dream of tasting beers and hitchhiking. Maybe these stairs would help him get there faster in the next life.

Once, when we were on poo duty, I made the mistake of teasing him about the trip, because the way he talked about it so much I figured he'd never actually go.

"Man, all that sounds like something you should have done *before* coming to a war zone," I'd told him.

"Citizenship," he said and shook his head.

"What?" I asked. Black smoke billowed from the giant metal drums as we stirred and poked the burning human refuse like witch's brew.

"I'm an 'alien,' gringo."

"Whoa," I said. I knew legal residents could serve even though they weren't citizens, but I'd never met anyone who'd put up a fight for a country that didn't even let them vote.

Sanchez yanked his stick out of the metal drum and stood back for a moment. Thick smoke trailed in a line from the end of the stick. Complaining about the smell was old news. "Until I get citizenship, I can't travel outside the country for very long," he said. "But after this tour Dobson, I can apply…and after that, I can take off. Anywhere."

"Where do you want to go?" I asked.

"Germany. A couple months there," he said. He sketched an outline of Western Europe in the dirt with the tip of the stick. Deutschland looked like a fat mushroom, France a sort of mauled star. "Then, at least a month in Paris." He drew the boot next, right down to the island of Sicily. "In Italy, I'll hike. Every inch of that leg." He laughed, then made a slow, grinding movement with his pelvis. "Right down to the tippy toe."

"Man, that's what I could use," I said. "What I wouldn't give to see a woman's legs about now."

"Tell me about it. Fucking pathetic," Sanchez said and jabbed his stick back into the poo barrel.

"You got anybody back home?" I asked.

"Funny, Dobson"

"No, serious, Sanchez. You got anybody?"

He grabbed another bucket of waste and poured it over the flames. "Did the President find Osama bin Laden yet?"

Sanchez would never know the answer to that now. We left

the air hangar and I carried the stairs across the base to a small conference room for memorial services. I set the stairs down and braced Sanchez's M4 against the back of the top step, barrel down. Then I balanced his Kevlar helmet on the buttstock of the gun and placed his boots on the first step.

"What do you think?" I asked Sanchez.

He still wasn't saying much, but I knew he could hear me. He stepped back to take a look, ghost-face expressionless as he stared at his own battlefield cross. After a minute, he took a knee and crossed himself, tucking his chin to his chest in silent prayer. As soon as I realized what Sanchez was doing, I looked the other way. Then I turned back, hoping he'd be gone. Instead, he walked over to the storage closet and started setting up folding chairs.

"It's not until tomorrow," I said. He fiddled frantically with the chairs, arranging them in perfectly symmetrical rows. "Sanchez?"

Nothing.

"SANCHEZ!" I yelled. "Hey! I'm sorry I left you in that river. I'm sorry you had to die like that. Sanchez, are you listening? I'm sorry about everything. Okay?"

He walked across the room and handed me a couple chairs, pointing to where they needed to go. I just stared at him, a mess of emotions clenched behind my teeth. If Sanchez felt anything at all, I couldn't tell.

That night on fire watch, Sanchez spilled it.

He paced back and forth along the lookout platform, restless as a junkie. He said he grew up in a church in Cuidad Juárez. "I could recite the 23rd Psalm by age five," he said. His voice sounded like a piece of sandpaper rubbed across a board. Without the harsh sunlight pouring through him, his form looked almost solid—a moving sculpture, battle rattle and all. "My father was a policeman," he said and scratched at his throat. "The Sinaloans decapitated him. We didn't even live in Juárez back then. We'd come from Tolentino for the day so Papa could take a test. He walked straight into a hold up at the Chihuahua Province headquarters. I never saw him again."

"Decapitated?"

"I also never saw Tolentino again. My mother took us to a Catholic church in Juárez. They kept me. She went home and got our stuff. Within a week, she was working in the colonias and I was in school with the nuns. Everything was free until my mother could save enough—hot dinners, blue collared shirts, dress shoes, school books, pencils…"

By the time my shift ended, Sanchez had described how his mother remarried and they moved from the church into the slums of Juárez. How he comforted himself hustling past gangs on his way to school, repeating psalms in cadence with each step. I tried to imagine Sanchez coming to America, his mother and stepfather chain-linking their bodies across the Rio Grande, water pressing hard against their shoulders as they navigated through the dark. Sanchez was seven years old, his sister Pilar just three months; his mother tied them to a plastic raft from Walmart along with two bags of belongings and then tied the raft around her husband's waist. Halfway across they heard a noise and knew someone was watching from the other side. "I had to keep quiet," Sanchez said. "It was either that or watch my own mother get shot." After that, they lived in Prado Verde, Texas, and tried to make a life.

The next morning, the Chaplain led the service for Sanchez. The only way to bounce back from something like that was to spend the rest of the day working up a sweat. I wanted to write a letter to Sanchez's family, but it would have to wait. I had my mind set on filling sandbags to line some outbuildings, and besides, I still had his ghost to contend with. I thanked the Chaplain and headed for the door. Sanchez looked hurt, but I couldn't talk to him with a bunch of Sergeants milling around the conference room. He followed me down the hallway, his presense pressing so close it felt like the current of a river impatiently shoving me along. I stopped and turned just before we got to the door.

"I guess this is it," I said. "For reals."

"Sorry?"

"I mean I guess this is goodbye, man, like *adios*."

A few soldiers exited the conference room and headed our direction. Sanchez backed off and started pacing again, balling his fists as if preparing to deliver an uppercut. One of the soldiers walked right through Sanchez's body, *whoosh*, completely un-phased. Sanchez flipped him the bird, then set his gaze on me. As soon as the guys closed the door behind them, Sanchez slammed my shoulders into the wall, his breath hot and dead against my face.

"You're not the one who says who says when it's *adios*," he said. "You're not the one."

"You've got to let go, Sanchez. You've got to move on," I said and squirmed away from him.

"Don't you think I'm trying?" he shouted. "Don't you think I'm exhausted?" I wanted to tell him to take it easy, that if he kept this up he would run himself ragged, but nothing made sense anymore.

Sanchez stayed with me for three more weeks. When I marched, he was at my heels, footsteps pounding like a second pulse. When I tried to sleep, he paced the perimeter of the bunkhouse, boots kicking up tiny clouds of dust. In the chow hall, he could hardly sit still. I watched as Sanchez darted between lines of soldiers, sniffing their food and peering over the servers' backs. The only place Sanchez wouldn't go was near water, which meant the bathhouse and shower room, and I realized his restlessness had nothing to do with me. Sanchez died by enemy fire, but whenever he talked about that night, he never mentioned the bridge. Not the bridge or the river or even the fact of how messed up his body looked after being under for so long.

His last night, Echo Company was mobilized north of the city toward the foothills. Our mission was to draw enemy fire, then see what we could light up, like walking into an ambush on purpose but bringing along enough firepower to blow those ragheads into the next country. Our convoy came within sight of the Kunduz and fanned out along the banks in 100-meter intervals. My platoon went first, anchoring five Humvees and a Bradley fighting vehicle at the northernmost point.

Sanchez sat crammed into the front seat, half of him over the driver's body, his other half over the gearshift. He kept talking into my ear, jibberish at times, other times clearer than spring water. The closer we got to the Kunduz, the more agitated he became. "My name is Ernesto Sanchez. I lived in the church, then in the city, then I crossed the Rio Grande." His eyes looked ragged, searching, like he couldn't get enough of whatever he needed to hold onto. But by then I understood his lingering didn't have anything to do with the here and now. Sanchez hurt for something on the other side.

My team exited the vehicle and got into position. I told Sanchez to hang tight but he was beyond listening. He stumbled from the Humvee, mumbling to himself, "...first in the church, then in the city, then I crossed the Rio Grande." He found me about fifty feet from our vehicle on the banks of the Kunduz, nestled behind a small cluster of rocks. The moonlight shone through his body as if through a curtain. Sanchez squatted next to me and began to whimper.

"Quiet down or you're gonna get us killed," I whispered, then realized my mistake. "Or you'll get me killed, man, whether those muj can hear you or not. You're messing with my concentration." I steadied my gaze through the NVG's and scanned the distant hills. For a moment, I wondered if it would be possible to shoot Sanchez—something, anything to help the guy out.

"I'm sorry," Sanchez wailed into the night. It was the kind of sobbing any soldier would feel embarrassed to see, and when he didn't let up, I socked him in the jaw.

Sanchez's breath caught. My fist had gone right through him, knuckles cracking into the rock. "Oh for fuck's sake, Sanchez," I said and grabbed my hand. That's when the mujahedeen zeroed in on us, four RPG's launched in quick succession from the other side of the river. I could see their tails arcing across the sky. One to my left, off target. Two to my right, the first coming up short, and the next pinned dead center on a team downriver. The fourth one gave me trouble. It didn't look in motion at all—just a fizzling, green ball of heat swelling in my field of vision.

I leapt from my position and rolled downhill, splashing into the river as the explosion shredded our Humvee into hot slivers of shrapnel. One of our guys called for a medic, and another hustled toward a neighboring team, an awkward limp to his gait. I braced myself against a boulder, the cool river wrapping around my body. For a moment, the valley fell quiet. I could hear Sanchez murmuring nearby: "My sister was so tiny...that river, so big." I heard the mechanical hum of our Bradley taking aim across the river, the turret readying to scissor 500 rounds a minute through enemy territory. Then, all at once, our teams lit up the hillside. It must have looked like the Armageddon to those muj, all of Echo Company taking aim at their unarmored camp.

I muscled my way out of the water and settled behind some shrubs. My M4 got waterlogged, but it didn't matter. The firefight ended in about two minutes. While everyone mounted up, I found Sanchez down the riverbank with his socks and boots off, wading up to his ankles in the Kunduz. He took another step and the water rose to his knees.

"Hey Sanchez," I called. "Sanchez?"

He turned to look at me. The moon was at his back, an awkward halo above his tear-stricken face. "First the church, then the city, then the Rio Grande…"

"Sanchez, I'm going to write that letter to your parents," I said. "It's time. And one to your sister, too."

"Pilar is dead," he said. He sounded like the real Sanchez then, the living, breathing soldier I'd known since the start of my tour. He took off his flak vest, then his helmet, dropping his battle rattle piece by piece into the river and watching it sink. "I held her hand on the raft in the Rio Grande. Her tiny hand, the one my mother told me to keep hold of until we'd made our crossing." He waded further, water coming up to the name stitched on his DCU's. "My stepfather pulled us and held onto my mother at the same time. He barely kept his head above water. Water sloshed onto our raft. I felt Pilar struggle. I had to bite the insides of my cheeks to keep from crying out. I held her hand. She died somewhere in between."

I didn't know what to say, and the next instant Sanchez was gone, joining the Kunduz as seamlessly as a drop of rain.

The next morning, I mounted up with some of the guys for the recon mission. The foothills looked so different in the early haze of dawn, and my mind felt quiet for the first time in weeks. Sanchez was gone. All I could do was hope he found some peace wherever he ended up. After a few minutes, I spotted the skeleton of our Humvee, its charred, steel arms jabbing awkwardly into the horizon. None of it looked salvageable, so we used the Bradley to crush the frame into the ground. I stood mesmerized on the banks of the river, watching that tank roll back and forth over the vehicle's remains, burying that tortured steel deep, deep into the sand.

CHECKPOINT

The guys and I had just finished setting up another checkpoint near the base in Basra when Sergeant Pike drove up in his Humvee, a team of rookies close behind. Despite his dough-ball cheeks, the man was more iron than grizzle, and he had a penchant for protocol.

"Private Dotson?" he barked.

"Yes, Sergeant?" I said.

"Private, I want you to set these cherries straight on the SOP for checkpoints, you hear?"

"Yes, Sergeant."

"They've been dicking around all morning, filling sandbags like we're on vacation in the Keys. How many bags can you fill in an hour, Private?"

"Thirty-seven."

"*Thirty-seven*," he said and gutted the new recruits with his gaze. "You hear that boys?"

"Yes, Sergeant Pike!" They shouted in unison, then hustled out of their vehicles and over to me. I don't know how long they'd been in country, but it couldn't have been more than 48 hours. I could smell the detergent on their DCU's. No stubble. No sunburns. Boys just old enough to vote.

"Anything else, Sarge?" I asked.

"Yeah. How about turning around?" Sergeant Pike said. I

looked beyond our checkpoint and saw a white sedan approaching slowly, a hundred meters in the distance.

We got into position and waited. So far, the rookies seemed to know what they were doing. Later, I'd tell them how to get on Pike's good side. For now, I had to help the sergeant make his point.

"We fire warning shots at 50 meters," I told the rookies. They took aim. The vehicle sputtered closer, and I landed a few shots just ahead of the bumper, then a handful to either side. Hunks of dirt and rock sprayed into the air. The car slowed to a halt. Its engine coughed until it fell silent.

Larson looked through his binoculars and reported, "Two male civilians, middle-aged. The driver's holding up his keys. I see both hands. The passenger's not doing anything. He's just sitting there—but I can't see his hands."

"If they get any closer, smoke 'em," Sergeant Pike said. He leaned against the barricade in the center of the road, polishing his sunglasses. He barely looked up.

One of the rookies, the tall one, said, "We've got movement." Sure enough, the driver lowered his hands, and a second later we heard the engine fire up. Slowly, they reversed the car and turned around, a snake-like line of dust following them all the way out of sight.

"All right, Suttons," the Sergeant said. He had a way of talking that commanded everyone's attention.

The tall rookie stood and looked at the Sergeant. "Yes, Sir?"

"You handle the next one," he said, then pivoted on his heels and headed back toward his Humvee.

Less than ten minutes later, Suttons had a job to do. A beat-up blue minivan came whirring down the dirt highway at about 35 mph. It neared the 50-meter mark in no time, and Suttons fired warning shots, mimicking the pattern he'd seen me shoot.

"One male civilian driver," Larson said. "One female in the passenger seat, younger. She's got her hands raised above her head. There's a rifle on the dashboard."

"Fire again," I ordered. We were all eyes and ears now, crouching alongside our vehicles, weapons aimed.

Suttons fired, blowing out a front tire. The van petered forward—cautiously but forward nonetheless. "I can see two passengers in the backseat," Larson said. "They're tiny; there's kids in there. Now the lady's hitting the driver. She's got a hold of his clothing."

The van continued forward. Forty meters. Thirty-five. Suttons aimed for the other tire, but missed. My buddy Chen aimed and nailed it, one hubcap flying in a silver arc across the road.

Twenty-five meters.

Twenty.

The van looked like a lumbering blue whale misplaced in the middle of the desert. I watched as it swerved left, then right, then left again.

"Larson, can you still see that gun?" I asked.

"It hasn't moved," he said. "They don't know what they're doing."

I'd seen this before and the outcome was never predictable. It could be a surrender. It could be someone with intel. It could even be a suicide mission.

"This is unbelievable," Suttons shouted. "Why don't they stop?"

"Just hold tight," I said. "Unless he touches that gun, all of you just hold tight a little longer."

Suttons panted like a dog at the end of its chain. I could feel the other rookies taking it all in—the van moving steadily closer, Suttons aiming through his scope, my orders to hold fire. In a flash, Suttons leapt to his feet and held his out palm, motioning the van to halt.

"No!" I shouted, but before I could explain the van sped forward and the other rookies rose to their feet, spraying a curtain of bullets at the vehicle.

Windows shattered into red-stained slivers of light.

Eight meters from our checkpoint, the van finally rolled to a stop.

The next few moments were lost to me. I must have shouted, must have grabbed Suttons by his unstained uniform and spit in his face, exploding breathlessly: "We're in Iraq! The sign for halt is a greeting. You put your hand up and people dash forward to meet it."

FIRST COMMANDER

The Americans guard everything, even their trash. But between Sadr City and the base at Camp Taji, you can still find trinkets if you're good at looking. My friend Ali is the best. One day, he even found a helmet with a photo of somebody's family sewn into the liner. We made a pretend soldier from the helmet and hid it in a shack, posed through a makeshift window. If you're driving by or in a hurry, it almost looks real.

Ali is still the best, but the day I found a ball of brand new parachute cord, all the boys danced around me like I was First Commander. I cut the rope into short pieces and made belts, trading with my friends for favors. Baahir swapped with me for a playing card he'd found and Naaji' for a piece of hard candy. Haamid ran all the way to the market and delivered me a chai. For this, I made him Second Commander, and we shared the rest of the rope. We strung old cloth and cardboard together and made forts all day.

Since the American invasion, we don't go to school. We watch the soldiers come and go and we imitate their toughness. Whenever they leave the base, we know if they want to pester or want to offer. It's easy to tell. When they want to offer, their trucks overflow with boxes sent especially for us. Their convoy stops and soldiers hop from vehicles to greet us. When they stand like that—feet spread, hands at the ready, the noonday sun angling at their backs—they look so tall and wide that just being next to them feels like resting in the shadow of a cloud. They wear so much armor you could drive a truck into them and they wouldn't even feel it. They're that strong.

Last week, they handed out bottles of water. When they do this, I'm lucky if I get one bottle. If I get two, I have to share. If somehow I get three, I'll be beat up so it's better not to try. No matter what, I have to run and push and holler with the other boys.

"Mister, Mister," I shouted, until finally, a soldier picked me from the crowd. He leaned over and handed me water. I took it and tore the cap off with my teeth, tilting my chin toward the sky to drink and drink. A warm wetness trickled through my body. It felt so good, like I was First Commander again, refreshed and ready for the next great battle.

PRESSIN' THE FLESH

My platoon's been at Camp Taji, Iraq for seventeen months. This week, our commanding officer picked 3rd and 4th Squads for a mission to press some flesh in Sadr City, which is his fancy way of telling us to go shake some hands and also his way of acknowledging we had our share of ambushes on night patrol and maybe a little humanitarian gesture would ease our attitudes.

We roll outside the wire for the short drive into the city, then turn off the main thoroughfare onto Nevada Street. Twenty-five of us fill the narrow road, Humvees idling and radios turned down. A few soldiers guard for snipers, but otherwise, no sweat.

I start handing out bottled water, and the Iraqi kids can't get enough. "George Bush!" they shout. "We love George Bush!" In less than five minutes, I've gone through eighty bottles of water, people dashing down the street to meet us, more hands reaching and reaching for whatever we can give. I'd like to be home right now, helping out my own family. My wife who still waits. My son who's mad as fire that I left.

The crowd swells, and I can barely hear myself think over their arguing. I haven't seen women and children for weeks, normal people just milling around as though an RPG couldn't career overhead any second and shred them all to bits. But still, something makes me edgy being this close to civilians. Any one of them could be the next suicide bomber, ready to make 3rd and 4th

Squads just a bunch of statistics.

"Mister! Mister! Give me chocolate!" an Iraqi boy shouts. He's probably eleven years old, shirtless with a pair of blue, tattered shorts, a piece of parachute cord tied through the belt loops. Last week, I gunned down two insurgents on this same street. I never even saw their faces. Today, I'm offering handouts to this bug-eyed haji kid, and chances are pretty good his dad rigs IED's along our patrol routes at night.

Don't ask me what I'm for or against. All I know is, I'm handing out bottles of water, and it isn't enough. Next thing, kids heckle me for chocolate. Fathers shout that they want their houses rebuilt. Mothers want hospitals. They all want their schools back. They want to know why they have to wait thirteen hours in line for gas while standing on top of the largest oil reserve on the continent. They want it all, and I don't have any of it.

Tell you the truth, after seventeen months I prefer the patrols. Looking through those night vision goggles, everything whittles down to two colors: green and black. If something moves wrong, if something lights up—I shoot it. Pretty simple. Pretty straight forward. Pretty goddamn free.

STARS OVER AFGHANISTAN

Ten years of war in Afghanistan and somehow Parsa's block remained relatively untouched in Kandahar. For once, living near a base seemed a blessing. During the hottest months, he and his family slept on the roof of their home to stay cool. This was for comfort more than tradition, but still, Parsa enjoyed the nightly task of passing his four sons one by one through the opening in their roof. Up top, his wife Yagana reached through the opening to assist, and for a brief moment, each child stood suspended between their parents, Parsa's hands around their waists and Yagana's tight-knuckled fingers wrapped around their wrists to pull them up.

Parsa climbed up last, swinging his legs to gain momentum for the final hoist through the narrow cut out. Task completed, he dusted off his hands and slid three strips of scrap wood over the opening. This would keep their youngest boy from toddling through the hole by accident. He still crawled, mostly, but Parsa refused to take chances. Four boys. Could God have blessed him any more than this? Parsa didn't think so.

One evening, Parsa passed his boys up to his wife and then he passed his rifle. Yagana leapt back at first, then curled her hands around the Russian-era Kalashnikov and pulled it through the opening.

"The children won't fall asleep if they see this," she told Parsa when he swung up onto the roof. "You'll scare them."

"Not as much as being helpless will scare them," Parsa said. "A wife should be thankful to her husband, not questioning."

She handed him the rifle and turned to the children, herding them for sleep.

Of course, Parsa knew that now more than ever the safety of his family lay beyond his control, rifle or not. NATO had been checking households around the base for three weeks straight. Last week, they rolled tanks down a street just four blocks away. Two nights ago, they raided his uncle's home, searching for a weapons cache. Tonight, who knew? Nobody got hurt during the raids, but Parsa resented the inevitable incursion. He refused to appear complacent.

He paced around the roof for half an hour, the rifle slung across his back. When he felt satisfied with the quiet, he slipped beneath the sheets and tucked the weapon alongside his leg. The sky overhead looked like a platter of stars, perhaps the only thing untouched by this war. To his right, the four boys rested like a row of perfectly stuffed grape leaves. To his left, Yagana exhaled her sleepy whistle, a warming kettle just before it's full-fledged boil.

Soon enough, a hollow *boom* echoed across the distant poppy fields. Then another, and another. Parsa reached for his rifle, sliding it into his arms as though in embrace. Those missiles had to be in Mandi Sar, maybe a little closer. Fifteen kilometers at the most. An electric orange hue arose in the southern sky and still, Parsa's family slept. He envied their peace.

It didn't last long. Within ten minutes, the entire family awoke, missiles falling in horribly predictable cadence. Parsa felt the house tremble beneath his back. Surely they weren't aiming for his district of Kandahar. Not with the base so close. Not with the absence of hostilities.

Next, a low, garbled rumbling erupted from the southern edge of the city and Parsa knew these were the tanks. The entire block shivered and even the stars overhead looked as though they might shake loose from the sky. Quickly, the family moved inside. First Yagana, then each boy passed through the opening, no ritual about it.

Parsa tossed the sheets down next and paused for a moment, listening for aircraft. He wasn't ready to leave. Not yet. "Come inside!" Yagana shouted. She could see him standing above the entrance, neck craned toward the sky. Parsa wanted one last look. His sky. His city. This place where he had done nothing wrong, his only dignity to protect his family—those boys—all the wealth and pride they would bring in years to come. Yagana reached for Parsa's ankles but he kicked her hands away and closed the opening, standing on top of the scrap wood. He loaded a magazine and took the gun off safety.

The tanks roared closer and Parsa saw the outlines of half a dozen helicopters in the distance. They moved in unison, a broad, metallic wave creeping over the city. Their spotlights shone like yellow tentacles tracing the lines of downtown streets. Parsa felt it then, as if those gigantic sky beasts could read his mind. He watched a light attack helicopter lower slowly over his roof, close enough that he could see the green lights in the cockpit. Parsa held his position, cradling the rifle in his arms as gusts from the chopper whipped his clothing against his body. Dust pelted his skin, his ears a raging symphony of heartbeats. What was he if not a man who could shield his family, against all odds, from this endless war?

Without explanation, the helicopter's spotlight flickered, then darkened completely. Just like that, the bird lifted away into the night. Within moments, the helicopters had realigned, steering for the west end of the city. Had they made some mistake? Parsa slumped to his knees, wind-chafed and alone in the sudden darkness.

DEUCE OUT

When we moved to Oregon four years ago, rain came with the lifestyle. Now it seemed a part of us. My brother Dustin wouldn't know what to make of the climate when he shipped out to Afghanistan. He'd be in the southern part of the country, near the Iranian border. We knew that much. But the sun burned long and hot there with sandstorms whipping across the plateau. I read about it once. How the storms move with such velocity that grains of sand push into every exposed millimeter of flesh. Fingernails, eardrums, nostrils, eyeballs. Tiny rocks needling beneath the skin that threaten infection, the slow death of any soldier.

Dustin left on a Tuesday morning at 1100 hours. I watched him settle behind the wheel of his Nissan Sentra and back down our driveway, wiper blades fanning across the windshield in a frenzied, farewell wave. Dad rode with him to the bus station in Newberg, just a few miles away. I trailed the sound of the muffler growing softer through the wet, winter morning, then turned toward the front door and braced myself for the sight of Mom. She'd be at the kitchen table or maybe the counter this time. Either way her expression stayed the same: face sagging around two eyes that looked right past you. Without Dustin around, I'd have to cope with her doom and gloom alone. I stepped into the house and pulled the door shut behind me. The latch clicked quietly into place, but by the way it sent shivers up my spine it could have been the pin of a grenade pulled free.

Dustin used to drop me off at school on his way to the community college, but now I was on my own. The Nissan sputtered and jerked as I grew familiar with the clutch. The defroster was broken again, and I struggled to see through the steamy windows. It made Newberg look like a town on the verge of collapse, a sinkhole waiting to happen. I hadn't even balanced my first algebraic equation of the day and it was already mid-afternoon in Afghanistan, the hottest part of Dustin's day. I parked in the student lot at 0800 hours and listened to the rain ping against the roof of the car. In the back of my mind I could hear Dustin coaxing me along: *Knock 'em dead, Sis.*

Before he left, I wanted to learn everything. Jingle trucks, battle rattle, fobbits, you name it. "C'mon. Spill it," I said.

"They don't teach you that stuff in basic, Steph."

"But you must have heard stories. You know. From your friends who've already been there." We lay on the grass in Harrison Park. The sun was out, the sky a fantastic blue we hadn't seen in months.

"No stories, Sis. Sorry."

"Okay, fine. What about from basic?"

Dustin feigned a yawn.

"Head's up!" someone shouted. I glanced in time to see a tall girl wave her arms and point overhead. Seconds later, a bright purple Frisbee landed near our feet. Dustin hopped up, flipped the disc in his palms once before uncoiling his arm in a perfect arc, fingertips letting go at just the right moment. We both watched as the flash of color streaked across the field. With a graceful leap, the girl snatched the Frisbee from the air and smiled.

"Thanks," she yelled.

Dustin bowed dramatically, then tipped forward into a full somersault, coming up on his toes and finishing with a wave.

"C'mon, show off," I said. "Let's go eat." I elbowed him hard in the ribs, and we both smiled.

"What'd you call me?" Dustin asked.

"Ladies man!" I said, and with that our race back to the car was on.

I didn't have to ask where he'd take us. The front booth at Round Table Pizza practically had a plaque with our names on it. They had the only self-serve soda machine in town, and I liked to mix and match.

"That's so gross, Sis."

"You haven't even tried it."

"Seven-Up and Dr. Pepper? Please." He slurped overflowing foam from the top of his A&W.

"Better drink it while you can," I said. "I read about those MREs you have to eat. And remember the chow they fed you in basic? You said that stuff made Mom's cooking look gourmet."

"Don't tell her I said that."

"Duh."

"And just because I'm stoked to go, doesn't mean I won't miss it here," he said.

"Yeah, right."

"You know what I mean, Sis. Not Newberg, but hanging out. Like this. You have to promise me you'll spend time with your friends. Or meet new people, I don't know—just don't hole up in the house and let Mom and Dad drive you crazy."

"Mom and Dad wouldn't notice either way," I said. "Besides, I'm almost graduated. It's not like I'm going to hang out in Newberg after that. People at school don't get me. You'd better write while you're gone."

Dustin bit into a slice of pizza and nodded. "Course I will." He reached across the table and took a sip of my mixed soda. "Not too bad, actually."

"At least here you get a first class D-FAC," I said.

"Steph. You're not in the Army, you know."

"D-FAC. It's a dining facil—"

"I know." Dustin shifted in his seat. "I know what it is."

That's when I started using military time. If Dustin found his new family in the Army, the least I could do was get the lingo down. At first it annoyed him, but once he shipped out it became our secret code. He told me things in letters home that Mom and Dad didn't know what to make of. Nothing top secret; just something we could call our own despite the fact that—excluding his basic training—I'd never gone more than a few days without seeing him my entire life.

The first email arrived four weeks after he left. Short and sweet. Typical Dustin. But the message included a P.S. for me: "Steph, look for something in the mail. Deuce out."

Deuce out. Our joke since we moved here from Indiana. It came from tennis, a game we never played. Our family got invited by one of Dad's new colleagues the week we arrived. We got lost driving there, unable to tell the difference between one gated community and the next, the illustrious West Hills unfolding beyond the town limits. Once we arrived, we knew we didn't belong, what with all the matching polo T-shirts and Jack Purcells.

"Isn't that a kind of car?" Dustin asked.

"*Jack Purcell?* No, dummy. It's a shoe. A really lame-ass, over-priced shoe," I said.

"Watch the swearing, Sis. We already stick out."

I stuck my tongue out at him. "You asked for it."

He rolled his eyes and grabbed me by the elbow. "Deuce out," he said and lead me down the bleacher steps, through the main gate, and into the courtyard. I laughed the entire way. "Deuce" had to do with scoring the match, but what it could possibly mean, we hadn't a clue. We were out of there. Both of us.

It felt funny at the time—funny enough to remain an inside joke for four years—but now, Dustin's words made me angry. How could he be so casual? I knew the Army had to be hard work, but being left behind felt even harder. A whole globe of possibilities existed beyond Newberg, and I couldn't reach any of them. Dustin's experience with other soldiers placed him into that same category: unreachable. He left and joined our nation's defenders. He saw new things, made new memories. I stayed stuck, waiting for graduation, doing whatever it took to avoid snapping at Mom every time I saw that glazed look on her face.

The surprise in the mail was a list of slang words used in Afghanistan. "It's short for now," Dustin wrote, "but I'm learning more everyday." *Hardball. DCU's. Ripped fuel.* Hardball meant any blacktop road, and Dustin wrote that he saw his last one when he took off from an airstrip on base in Kuwait. DCU stood for desert camouflage uniform, apparently nothing special. "Imagine wearing faded brown fatigues every day from head to toe. I feel like the effing UPS driver, Sis, trust me. You're not missing out." The last one surprised me: ripped fuel. It's the way soldiers talked about over-the-counter fad pills, squandered and traded in combat like candy. "Anything to amp your energy," Dustin wrote. "Walking with 50 pounds of battle rattle on, let alone going out on patrol, is workout enough in this heat."

But by spring, letters from Dustin rarely came. The leader of his unit's Family Readiness Group told us not to take it personally.

"Many soldiers find the support they need within their own platoon," the leader said. "Life is complicated over there." As if things didn't feel complicated here. I watched Mom sink further into the couch. She hardly even noticed that I skipped Senior Prom. Dad didn't turn mean, but some part of him stayed held back. My senior year of high school, yet everything deepened into a dull-colored silence that made me feel like a ghost in my own house. All I wanted was for someone to shout orders in my face—anything to break the silence with some clear directions. It had to be easier than slogging alone through the blandness of waiting back home.

Whenever Dustin's letters came, I searched the envelopes for signs of the desert. I knew his mail went through a collection point in Kabul before processing. Once stateside, it might even be X-rayed before making its way into the hands of a US postal worker, then finally delivered to our box. I don't know what I expected. Dust, sand, a fingerprint—but even his brief, handwritten pages felt lifeless. "Hotel, Sierra Hotel," Dustin wrote. I knew that he meant HSH, using the Army's phonetic alphabet to say, "Home, Sweet Home," a place he said he missed, though I found that hard to believe. I wanted to tell him the only thing he was missing would be my high school graduation, which couldn't seem to come fast enough.

"We don't even know where he is," Mom whimpered one night. We sat on the couch with our TV dinners, watching the evening news.

"He's over there," Dad said and pointed his fork at the lower half of an Afghanistan map on the screen.

"But, Pete." She sighed. "We don't even know what he's doing."

"He's an infantryman. He's doing his job. He's doing what the Army trained him to do."

"And what, exactly, is that?" she asked. She rarely talked that way.

Dad pressed the mute button on the remote, then dropped his fork into a rubbery pile of Salisbury steak and gravy. "Let's go out. Do you want to go out? What do you say? Ice cream? Steph?" He stared straight ahead, the blue light of the television casting his face in electric plaster.

"Sure, Dad."

"Fine," Mom said. "I'll eat double. For Dustin. God knows my boy deserves a scoop of chocolate ice cream by now."

"*Our* boy," Dad said. But I said it too and they both looked at me.

"*Our* boy," I repeated. "You two aren't the only ones that miss him."

I started training the next morning, 0715 hours, 26 MAR 10. Dustin offered me his free weights before he left but I never bothered to pick one up. They came in handy now. I jammed a sweatshirt into the bottom of my Jansport for padding, then set a fifteen-pound weight on top. I wrapped the matching weight in my gym shirt and crammed that, along with my textbooks and binder into my pack. It looked awkward but did the job.

"I'm going to work," Mom called from downstairs.

"I'll catch the bus," I said. The Nissan was in the shop. I didn't care. It made me miss Dustin too much. A few minutes later I hustled down the stairs, faster than normal from the weight bearing down on me, then out the front door. I hit the pavement at a slow jog, heart pounding. Two hundred meters to the bus stop and I'd already broken a sweat.

Every day after school I had two hours to workout before Mom and Dad got home. I found out about the Army's first physical fitness test online. It seemed simple enough: two minutes of sit-ups, two minutes of push-ups, and a timed two mile run. I knew I could do it, but whether or not I could nail enough repetitions or hit the sweet spot with my running pace seemed another matter. One way to find out.

Once I made up my mind about enlisting, I thought time would zip past. Instead, the opposite happened. 1545 hours. 15 APR 10. A date everyone else remembered because of taxes. I remember because it was the first time I set foot in the U.S. Army Recruiting Office.

I wore my hiking boots—the closest thing I owned to combat boots—with a pair of Dustin's ratty, beige cargo pants, my dark gray hoodie, and my Jansport (still with the free weights in it). I kept my hair pulled tight in a ponytail, not a single dark brown strand fallen loose along the back of my neck. My bangs distracted from the look, but I clipped them to one side and sprayed them down. From the driver's seat of the Nissan I saw storefront displays plastered with soldiers of every race. I cracked my window and squinted through the rain. The left side of the display featured the latest military protective gear, DCU's, and training fatigues. The right side encased two life-sized cardboard cutouts of the same soldier—one in uniform with a M4 Carbine at his side, another in a cap and gown, gripping a leather-encased diploma. I checked my hair in the rearview, then hustled from the car to the main door, leaping over puddles in between.

My boots squeaked with every step, a line of sole-shaped puddles following me down the linoleum hallway. I turned right into the U.S. Army entrance—there were others, one for each branch of the military—and snapped my feet and hands to attention. The drumming of my heart could have kept time for an entire company. I stilled my breath and straightened my spine. I didn't know how to salute and didn't dare try, but I'd studied the grades online and observed that the first man I saw wore a patch with three hard stripes.

"Good afternoon, Sergeant," I said.

"Good afternoon, Ma'am. What can I do for you today?"

"I'd like to enlist. My brother is in Afghanistan. I've been working out. I want to sign up," I said. Then I bit the inside of my cheeks to make myself shut up.

I tried to hold the Sergeant's gaze but grew too curious. Three other desks filled out the tiny office, two more male non-commissioned officers and one woman, each wearing full fatigues. The American flag hung above the Oregon flag. Beneath them both I saw a signed photo of President Obama, Commander in Chief.

The Sergeant smiled and looked at the others. "Congratulations," he said. "That's a decision you should be proud of. Sergeant Hill?"

"Yes, Sir?" the woman answered.

"Please get Ms.—"

"Bowlin," I said.

"—Ms. Bowlin oriented."

"Yes, Sir." She turned and indicated that I sit in the empty chair next to her desk. "Welcome to the family, Ms. Bowlin. I can tell already the Army will be pleased to have you."

Sergeant Hill explained a packet of promotional materials, then gave me a fact sheet to show my high school guidance counselor. As a minor without a degree, I needed proof I was on track to graduate high school in good standing. Easy enough. More difficult would be what Sergeant Hill called PC, parental consent. My 18th birthday wasn't for another five weeks, 24 MAY

92.

"With all due respect, Ma'am, I'd prefer not to tell my parents I'm enlisting. At least, not until I get to go to basic."

"That'll be fine, Ms. Bowlin. We can get your information into our system this afternoon," Sergeant Hill said and began entering my name into the computer database. "But we can't get you started in our Future Soldier Program until you're 18 or have PC."

"I can train on my own while I wait," I said. I almost unzipped my pack to show her the weights but decided against it.

"Is there a particular career in the Army that interests you?"

"I want to work in combat support."

Sergeant Hill paused at her keyboard and looked at me. "Then physical training is a good idea, Ms. Bowlin."

I waited for her to smile but she didn't. "What else can I do in the meantime?"

She stood and opened a file cabinet, retrieving a thick pile of papers. "This," she said, slapping the heavy stack onto her desk, "is a packet of five practice tests for the ASVAB."

"The—?"

"The Armed Services Vocation Aptitude and Battery test. It's like the SAT at an 8th grade level."

"I've taken the SAT."

"That's a good start," she said and handed me the practice tests. "But this will test you for various career fields as well."

I left two hours later with a free ARMY T-shirt and more papers than I could fit into my Jansport. Most importantly, I had a glossy appointment card stamped for the day after my birthday, 0900 hours. I'd bring my letter of good standing and take the ASVAB right there at the Recruiting Office. Three days later I'd find out if I scored high enough and which career fields I was slated for. With everything in place, I could be in Portland at the

Military Entrance Processing Station (MEPS) by 01 JUN 10 for my physical, then take my Oath of Enlistment.

By the time I pulled the Nissan into our driveway, Mom was already home from work. I finally felt excited about something for the first time since Dustin left. I wanted to rush inside and tell Mom about the enlistment grades and education benefits, the latest cash bonuses since Obama upped the troops in Afghanistan. But she wouldn't understand. The way that I saw it, Dustin and I were two of the most loyal siblings on the planet. I didn't want to do anything without him and not even the global war on terror could prevent me from trying to maintain that. I would go and be with him. Even if we never ended up in the same province, at least I could say I was there. I tried. He wouldn't be the only Bowlin soldier choking on desert sand.

A letter from Dustin arrived 23 MAY 10, two days before my appointment for the ASVAB. It included a Kodak memory card from his digital camera, which explained why the letter was dated April, but it hadn't arrived until late May. An officer in Kabul probably screened the images first. We'd never know how many Dustin originally sent, but when I loaded the photos onto the computer in my bedroom, we only saw seven. Mom and Dad peered over my shoulder and waited as I enlarged each image.

The first two looked blurry: accidental shots of a soldier's boot and another of somebody's back. But the third picture showed a close-up of Dustin with six other Privates in his unit, each standing shoulder-to-shoulder, eyes squinting into the sun. Dustin's face looked darker than I'd ever seen it, either from sand or sunburn or a mix of both. His eyes blazed brilliant green beneath the rim of his helmet. Behind him, the desert looked as spent as a piece of old cardboard.

The next picture must have been a joke, because there were four Privates crossing a dirt road, Dustin leading the way, then two other soldiers on the sidelines laughing and pointing at them.

"It's *Abbey Road*," Mom said. She almost smiled.

"What?" I asked.

"*Abbey Road*, honey. The Beatles album."

"Huh?"

"See how they're spread evenly across the road, toe-to-heel?" Dad pointed to the picture. "And that one there, the third guy—he has a cigarette in his hand."

"Yeah?" I was still confused.

"Look, Pete," Mom said. "Dustin even put his hands in his pockets, just like Lennon."

"Oh yeah," Dad said. He smiled after he spoke, a wide, fatherly grin I hadn't seen in a while.

"Isn't John Lennon the guy who got shot?" I asked.

Mom glared at me, then turned abruptly and left the room. Dad waited for a moment and exhaled a long breath. "Yes, Stephanie. John Lennon was assassinated."

"Dad, I didn't mean to—"

"I know. Just try think about how your mother feels right now, okay? Try to think about it." He left my room and took Dustin's letter with him. I skimmed the last few pictures, but they only showed soldiers I didn't know, hulky guys holding M16's up to the camera. They looked tough, but they also looked bored. I didn't notice any women.

When I heard Mom and Dad close their bedroom door for the night, I reached under my mattress and pulled out the Army materials Sergeant Hill offered my very first day. I visited her a few times since, and she shared study tips with me. She told me to call her Corrine and gave me her cell phone number in case I had any last minute study questions. Even though I couldn't technically join the Future Soldier Program until I'd passed all my tests, Corrine liked my enthusiasm and gave me handouts each time I stopped by the Recruitment Office.

The Seven Army Values loosely spelled the word "leadership," which helped me remember them in order: Loyalty, Duty, Respect, Selfless Service, Honor, Integrity, and Personal Courage. The Soldier's Creed read like a prayer, which is exactly how I recited it to myself each night: *I will always place the mission first. I will never leave a fallen comrade. I am a guardian of freedom and the American way of life. I am an American Soldier.*

2300 hours. 24 MAY 10. The day Dustin would have taken me to Round Table Pizza for my birthday, if he hadn't left, and let me order Canadian bacon and pineapple. My favorite. His least. Instead, I sat in bed writing my third draft of a letter to him, trying to find the best way to surprise him with my enlistment. Now he wouldn't be the only one. The Army would be one more thing we could share, something bigger than Newberg and bigger than our inside jokes. It would also be my ticket to something better than home. The thought alone made me smile. "I'm on my way," I wrote. "Can't wait!"

The next day, I wore my Army shirt to take the ASVAB and kept Corrine's business card in my wallet for good luck. I had to skip school, but by then it didn't matter. In less than a week I'd be a high school graduate, one step closer to Dustin. I wanted to qualify for as many career fields as possible. Combat support would be the closest to infantry work I could get—women weren't allowed in full combat. From what I could tell, I'd probably be assigned maintenance or civil affairs work in the field.

28 MAY 10. 1300 hours. Corrine's name flashed on the caller ID on my cell. I was in Chem class but called her back during passing time.

"Corrine? Hey, it's Steph. I'm sorry I couldn't pick up."

"That's understandable."

"Excuse me, hold on. Can you hold on?" I ducked through the hallway and quickly spun the combo on my locker. "Corrine, are you there?"

"Still here." She chuckled to herself.

I stuck my head into the locker and pressed the phone tightly to my ear. A river of students flowed down the hall behind me but I could have been in a foxhole, the enemy all around. My heart raced with anticipation. "Sorry. It's a little noisy right now."

"That's fine, Stephanie. This will only take a minute. We received the results of your ASVAB test this morning, and I'm proud to say you passed with flying colors. I'd like to see you at your earliest convenience to get you over to MEPS and set you up with a career counselor."

"Sweet!" I shouted. "I mean, thank you, Sergeant." The bell rang and the hallway emptied. I pulled my head from my locker and reset the lock. "I'll report at 1500 hours."

"That'll be fine, Steph." Then she hung up.

I stared at the phone in my hand. Something was actually happening. I would be a soldier in the US Army. The tardy bell rang, and I hustled into the girls' bathroom. I should have been in English, but that seemed worlds away. Finals were over, and teachers held parties in class, checking in textbooks and handing out doughnuts. I set my backpack on the floor, lowering the forty pounds with ease. Standing in front of the large mirror, I backed my left arm out of my sweatshirt sleeve and through the bottom, raising my arm like a body builder. I flexed my muscles and tightened my fist. Corrine had told me that soldiers use their fists as a guide for reading topographical maps, the top line of my knuckles like a ridge of mountains. Between each knuckle, a saddle, and at the edge of my fist along the side of my pinky was a cliff. Hills could be marked on either side of each knuckle, the places where soldiers had to climb or descend near the summit of each knuckle-peak.

Things moved quickly after that. The career counselor said they could only reserve my Army job for seven days, then I had to decide. I knew right away I wanted to be a Bridge Crewmember, position 21C. A few days later I drove to the MEPS office in Portland to swear in and take the Oath of Enlistment. Job description and contract in hand, I settled into the driver's seat of the Nissan to drive home and tell Mom and Dad. That's when my phone rang. It was Dustin. I held the sound of his voice in the palm of my hand, the closest we'd been in almost six months.

"Steph, it's me I—"

"Dustin? Where are you?" I almost shrieked. "You're not going to believe this! I just finished—"

"What do you think you're doing?" He sounded like a stranger. Worse. He sounded like Dad, the few times I'd heard him lose his temper.

"Steph, I got your letter."

"Dustin, I passed. I passed everything. Or at least the beginning of everything. It's all happening!"

"This isn't for you. This isn't what it seems," he said. Then slowly: "You. Do not belong. In the Army."

"What do you mean I don't belong? I just took my Oath. We can be in it together, now. So much has happened since you left. I'm going to be a Bridge Crewmember. We might even be in the same—"

"Goddamnit, Sis. Slow down!" I heard his lungs heave, his voice crack. "There's nothing you can do for me here."

"Dustin?" I said his name, but it got lost somewhere over the Pacific. He wasn't the same brother I had before he left. Then again, I wasn't the same sister.

"I gotta go," he said. "I'll email you later."

After basic, I shipped to Fort Leonardwood, Missouri, for bridge training. By 20 SEP 10 I flew to a US Army base in Germany for TTP. Tactics, techniques, and practices. I sent letters to Mom and Dad once a month, short and sweet—just like Dustin's.

For his part, Dustin called almost every week. He never got angry with me like that again, but we rarely talked about my enlistment. He hated feeling responsible, and nothing I said convinced him I'd done it for myself as much as for him. We didn't joke around like before, but at least our military jargon finally had a true purpose. The daily B.S. of unit power struggles, trying to swipe the right kinds of protective gear, downing MREs between gags—I lived all of it, and all of it brought us more and more into our new family. We served in the same Division but never crossed paths in the field. He couldn't see how hard I worked, but very few women served in combat support and word got around. I could hold my own, at least at first, and that's the message I wanted him to hear.

02 FEB 11. I landed in Kabul and began the long road trip to Kunar Province in eastern Afghanistan. We were there to erect a series of dry support bridges used for crossing land gaps. About the time Dustin flew home on leave—he joked it was "spring break"—my Company moved to Nuristan Province in the Hindu

Kush Mountains. There was heavy fighting along the Pakistan border and infantrymen needed temporary bridges for transport. Something that could be set up and dismantled in a hurry. We were trained to build modular bridges in under ninety minutes.

We rarely left a bridge set up overnight, as the open crossing created a liability—an invitation for insurgents. But the sun had set, and we had another unit that needed to cross at the same location in a few hours. Guards posted on either end and the rest of us set up camp strategically tucked into sidewalls of the mountain. 0230 hours, 26 APR 11, a handful of insurgents tried to cross the bridge. They made it halfway before being detected, and when they returned fire, our combat soldiers took them out. We dismantled the bridge that day, but by nightfall more insurgents crossed the land gap without it. Never mind how they navigated those cliffs by hand and foot, but they did, and they ambushed our camp just before sunrise.

The gunfire sounded like microwave popcorn at first. I'd never been that close to it before. At least not when it was aimed at me. I woke disoriented, snapped on my Kevlar, grabbed my flack vest, and got onto all fours. Right arm through the first hole, left arm through the second. Bullets sang by my ears, no time to zip. I grabbed my weapon, then ran low and straight, following the sound of our soldiers' voices. Watch how fast I ran, the open flaps of my vest like wings in the wind. See how the bullets danced around me, never hitting their target. Then finally, half a dozen of them did.

0439 hours. 27 APR 11.

I have nothing to say about white lights or Heaven or Hell or even who else I saw. But I will say this: there's nothing like it, that fever of live-action death.

In the living world, people study amputees with ghost limbs.

A missing right arm mysteriously itches. A missing left leg throbs. In the dead world, we're given ghost ears. Different people hear different things. What I hear is always the same. It's Mom. It's Dad. They keep asking, "What happened? What happened? What happened?"

THE WAITING: PART I

Now there's waiting to get deployed and there's waiting to get shot at. The first one feels like a weeklong constipation, except it's usually more than a week, and when we finally do get called, there isn't time to take a dump anyway. The second one feels exactly how it sounds. We're sitting there as bored as heifers since we can't engage unless fired at, then *pop*, some haji gets the notion to ready-aim-fire, and we're all balls and bulls. On again off again. Enough highs and lows to make a man forget which way's up.

Then there's waiting in lines. Lines for chow and lines for mail call. Lines for the phone so long the war might finish before we dial home. Lines for weapons inspection, roll call, issuing ammo. More lines for TB shots, anthrax vaccines, Hepatitis, typhoid fever. Next up: SARS and swine flu vaccines, Tetanus shots, malaria pills—you name it, we've got it in our veins.

On the way home, there's waiting at every border. In Kuwait, we wait—decompression seminars, post-deployment paperwork, weapons returns, Army-issued gear checks. Then waiting again on a different plane. Stateside, we debrief and demobilize, dress down for another med check and study up on combat stress, reunion stress, post-traumatic stress. We squirm through the suicide brief last, so stressed about being stressed we can't wait any longer to get gone and de-stress.

But at home, there's waiting to see if the kids still love us, the wife. We're different now. We know what we're capable of. From here on out, it's waiting to see if we can make two worlds meet without getting lost in between.

THE WAITING: PART II

We don't like to talk about the waiting very much, since talking about it means thinking about it and thinking about it does us in. But if you want to know, it feels like we're all being held underwater. We can hold our breath just fine. It's not knowing when we get to come up for air that makes it hard.

Claire schedules the appointments at her salon in military time. Heather is training for a marathon. Melissa started a daycare to help the moms on base, and Cheryl works like a professional carpooler, carting everybody's kids from hockey practice to tap lessons and home again. Eddie has it real different—his wife's over there as an MP. He's got the kids and keeps to himself, but he'll lend a hand when needed. Never makes us feel incapable about it, either.

We stick together, that's what it is. It's our blood over there too. Seems like we're doing just as much bonding back home as they're doing over there. Just of a different nature. And we call each other a lot. Like making sure at 6 o'clock we're on the phone, so we don't turn on the television and listen to more of that bad-news-IED-no-further-details kind of talk.

When they come home, they won't be the same. We'll have to love them differently. It'll be our turn to fight, each of us on the front lines of a private war.

THEY CALL US CHERRIES

They call us cherries, rookies, freshies. They say back off, chisel in, knuckle down, cowboy up. If you goof and start yapping about the first time you almost got gutted, guys'll slam your back into the wall and tell you: Keep it glued. We don't talk about near misses.

If you're lucky, one will like you enough—maybe you're from the same state or both dig the Red Sox, maybe both your moms are Irish. That guy will give you tips. Check your laces, he'll say before inspection. Shave closer, scrub faster, talk less. Not like that, like this. Not later, now. Oh, and that? Not ever.

There on out, it's a matter of whether what you bring outweighs what you draw. Dawson's quick-witted with his tongue but stupid as a buckshot fawn when we're on patrol. He makes our First Sergeant laugh at just the right time though, saving our virgin hides at least once a week. Sandhill can run a 5K, shit, and shave before first chow, then hoist sandbags till sunset if he has to. Only trouble is, his mouth is his motor. He can't do a thing unless he's talking. Talk your ear off if you're not careful, leave you dizzy and deaf two hours later.

One kid cried his first night in country. So young he still had pimples. He slept holding an undershirt like a snot rag to his face. "Stupid, stupid, stupid, stupid," he said, blubbering away in his bunk. By morning, his eyes looked half-shut from all the gushing. Then on out, they called him Young & Stupid. C'mere, Young &

Stupid, pick up this ammo I dropped. C'mere, Young & Stupid, I need you to lick my ass cheeks clean. C'mere, Young & Stupid, there's a new chokehold I want to practice.

We're not off the hook until the next rookies enter the ringer. We watch them with gratitude and hatred. We say, welcome cherries. They look at us, wondering about the odds of making it home scratch-free. We laugh. Hope is just a gravestone in this cemetery of a war. "Not a chance," we say. "Not a chance in hell."

I TOLD THEM

I told those boys I'd climb them like a ladder. I told them I'd make their mothers sorry. I told them next time one of them fell asleep posting fire watch, he'd meet me in his nightmares. I told them once I finished with them, they'd be defecating from their mouths for a week. That once I finished with them, I'd start in on their sisters. I told them this wasn't frat boy hazing, this was shock and awe, so clamp down and man up for the taste of their own severed tongues sliding down the backs of their throats.

When they grew tired, when they thought they were done, I said this is the marathon, boys. Mile *numero uno*. Uphill the rest of the way. I told them the only thing hotter than this kind of Hell is the tip of my dick pumping into their puckered assholes.

Once, I told them nothing at all: zero dark thirty, me and the other first sergeants hustled into the barracks and choke-tied those rookies like homicide victims. Most of them just had thermals and hats on, nothing on their feet. We hustled them through the frigid, black night into the training woods. Spun them around. Poured whiskey in their eyes. We left them to nose their way back in time for formation and then we did it again. If it was light out, we blindfolded them. When it grew dark, we rigged spook-traps in the woods.

When they couldn't tell their own peckers from a pack of ammo, we loaded them up, battle rattle and all. Kevlar, flak vests, gas masks, weapons, and then some. They stood at attention in full fatigues, a perfect blending of greens and browns.

I told them now, boys, now you belong to me.

AASEYA & RAHIM

Rahim earned 30 *afghanis* from the Taliban for each NGO supply truck he intercepted. In Oruzgan province, the trucks came intermittently, but Rahim would not, God willing, work to win nothing, and he would not, God willing, live to lose everything. On slow days, he walked the dry creek beds outside town, shoveling mud for brick- making. Before the Taliban, Rahim labored for an Oruzgan warlord, harassing nomadic clans when their presence became a nuisance to parties vying for the warlord's blessing. And during the Soviet invasion, he worked for the Afghan National Army, training young recruits in weapons maintenance. Before that, he was a boy, and that was another story.

But more and more, Rahim's pay came late. At first, after every truck he successfully intercepted. Then, every few weeks. One month, the Taliban paid Rahim in *rupees*. His wife Aaseya fingered the coins suspiciously in her palms. *Rupees* came from Pakistan, where the fiercest Taliban had fled: the ones who shamed women beyond the burqa, beyond imprisonment. The ones who, when they weren't hiding, gathered stones for pelting or recruited children from the streets. How could she use coins that came from those men? Then again, if she refused and those men were still in Tarin Kowt, she'd be fingerless on one hand for her defiance.

Aaseya had begun to love Rahim for his resourcefulness. At first, she didn't love him for anything because she didn't know him. Only now, four years into their prearranged marriage, did Aaseya feel herself start to blend with Rahim: how she anticipated his return from the highways each afternoon, how she noticed his scent as she washed his keffiyeh. She admitted to herself she liked his touch sometimes, a firm, hot hand sifting through the folds of her shalwar kameez. "God willing?" he'd ask, the pleasant shock of his lips on hers. "God's will is busy," she sometimes said, this freedom of refusal—she understood—only hers because of Rahim's past. Indeed a rare refusal in Tarin Kowt, in Oruzgan, in all of her country.

One morning, Aaseya curled the *rupees* into her fist and ducked out of their apartment, headed for the bazaar. Heat clung to her like a second skin. She shifted the fabric on her burgundy headdress so it splayed open at the sides, inviting a warm breeze. Sunlight warmed her face, her hands, the soft skin around her ankles. Gazing down the main thoroughfare, Aaseya thought: bread, chickpeas, maybe some ghee to make a sweet halwau later that week.

She heard the sounds of the bazaar several blocks away. It would be mostly women at this hour and the women never said much. They busied themselves with their sons, their unending tasks as mothers. But there were animals for slaughter and children who begged rudely, their bone-thin backs pressed against the posts of bazaar tents. "Assalaamu alaikum," or, more difficult to bear, the simple, repeated incantation: "Allah. Allah. Allah." She could conjure their tinny voices from the depths of sleep if she had to.

Past the music shops with CD's hanging like prayer flags. Past row after row of hand-woven rugs and tapestries, collapsible wooden bowls, and ornate hookas. Just beyond the displays of stone plates and vases, a closet-sized bookstore perched on the corner. Aaseya walked slowly with her satchel of groceries, eyeing the shop first from across the street, then boldly walking to the display window. She had about ten seconds before her lingering might draw suspicion. Tarin Kowt was no longer under Taliban rule and though her husband knew she was an educated young woman, she was a woman still and unaccompanied at that. She glimpsed a few bright paperbacks, a stack of local papers, and there—right there—words she knew in English: *The New York Times*.

Half a globe away, America handed out cash bonuses to new enlistees in the U.S. Army. Six grand if you had college credits to your name. A few more if you bought a house. Sign here, test there, take the money, and we're on the move. Thirty thousand troops packed for Afghanistan in the latest surge, battle rattle and all.

Which might have explained why, after being paid in *rupees*, the following week Rahim was paid in U.S. bills. Now Aaseya knew about the money for certain. All the locals in Tarin Kowt knew. U.S. Colonels had come with cash in hand to put warlords on payroll in exchange for intelligence about various clans in their provinces, sometimes Taliban, other times defectors from the Afghan National Army. The Colonels wanted addresses of safe houses. They wanted dates and names. Warlords hired willing Afghan men to report such intelligence and now, Aaseya believed, her husband's wages came from a Taliban soldier who worked for a U.S.-paid warlord by day and shot rocket-propelled grenades at the Multi National Army base by night.

It went something like this: the warlords in Oruzgan understood what the U.S. Colonels could not. "Keeping the peace" was a relative term, something that changed from one day to the next and did not apply to hours after sunset. The most effective way for a warlord to guarantee safe passage of U.S. troops through his province was to bribe local Taliban with enough cash to keep them from planting IED's or ambushing a convoy. Meantime, the same Taliban hired locals like Rahim to heckle NGO supply trucks trying to reach refugee camps south of the city. The Taliban reasoned that soon enough, joining their cause would look better than the camps, better than begging, and better, even, than piecemeal work for the Americans, whose corner of the base by now employed several hundred Afghans daily to keep things up and running. Rahim reasoned his best work lay somewhere in the middle, and getting paid in U.S. bills was surely nothing to complain about.

"So your boss has been promoted," Aeseya said.

Rahim slid the U.S. bills back into his vest and sat on the floor, waiting for his supper. "I wish you wouldn't joke about it like that." He watched Aaseya's shoulders shift as she stirred pilaf on the stove.

"It's not a joke to me," she said. "You know what this means."

"It means I'm working for a man who works for more than one side, Aaseya, and in Afghanistan that means nothing."

"It means everything."

"Say it directly."

"It means he will just as easily betray you as he betrays his own." She turned when she said it, looking at Rahim with a kind of stiffness he had not seen before. Affection or a threat? Four years and still, he felt he didn't know her. Obstinate? Yes. Intelligent? In a limited way. But to *know* her seemed impossible to Rahim. He stood and walked toward the pantry. Aaseya resumed stirring. When she turned to reach for a bowl, Rahim was at her back.

"You've forgotten these," he said and handed her a tin of raisins. She took them from him gently and then he knew. For the first time since the U.S. invasion, his wife feared for his safety. He brought his lips to her ear, his hands to her shoulders. "Aaseya, I am nothing in this war," he said. "I work for myself. I am not owed to anyone."

Rahim had been owed to many people as a child, sold out of poverty to a wealthy merchant in Kabul to be trained in singing and dancing for the mujahedeen generals. They called the practice *batcha bazi* and Rahim's parents were promised their boy would be fed, rested, and even paid when his skills matured. The generals took from him like a tray of appetizers. In truth, there were two Rahims. The boy before *batcha bazi* and the boy after. This Rahim—the Rahim now talking into his wife's ear, listening for a quickening or stilling of her breath, remembering what fear was like himself—had been returned to his parents at sixteen. By that age, dancing boys were of no interest to the generals, the sex a far cry from the innocence they craved.

"Save them for later," Aaseya said.

"The raisins?"

"Yes." She smiled, remembering the newspaper in the shop window. "They're for a special sauce. For our halwau."

"With raisins?" He looked at his wife, this stranger in his kitchen.

"Rahim!" She turned into him and smiled. "You are always ruining the surprise."

For her part, Aaseya had been lucky to stay married at all. Afghanistan had little tolerance for women who never bore children. Her inability to conceive with Rahim raised questions about her fertility, a near death sentence in her country, but none of this was discovered until after their wedding and of course, its consummation. There should be one child for every year of marriage, at least initially. For Aaseya, that would have meant four by age twenty, each of them crowding the tiny apartment, sickening her with work and worry. Being childless was one of many things that set Aaseya apart. Another, of course, was at the back of this surprise: she wanted to return to school. Call it bribery. Call it ritual. A sweet dessert with special raisin sauce might help, and Aaseya wasn't above steering her husband's favor one way over another.

She returned to the bazaar the next morning. A young boy stood across the street from the bookstore, begging. Aaseya didn't hesitate.

"Here," she said and showed the boy a U.S. dollar bill.

His round eyes swelled. "Miss?" He looked afraid to take it, the amount so large it must be a trick.

And it was, in a way. She helped the boy to his feet, turned him about for inspection, and dusted off his clothing with a few firm swipes of her hand. She knelt down and looked into his eyes. "There's a newspaper in the window. I want you to buy it and bring it to me." She pressed the dollar into his sweaty hand.

"Which one?" the boy asked. This was good. She might be able to trust him.

"In the window. Just say *New York*. Can you say it in English? *New York*."

He tried. He was younger than she thought. It sounded off.

Nu wok. Nu wok. It would have to do.

"Fine," she said. "Say that and point to it. The one in the window."

The boy nodded and she took his hand as they walked across the street, the money pressed between their palms. At the corner, he fled through the shop door, bells ringing behind him. Aaseya waited alone on the dusty sidewalk. It was her fortune to find this boy here on this morning, it had to be. And, if God willed it, it would be her fortune to study freely again as well.

She gazed at the sky, cloudless and pale blue. Mourning doves balanced on power lines overhead. The birds looked dull, brown; the same color as the dirt beneath Rahim's fingernails after a day working creek beds. The same color as the alleys, the side roads, the brick walls that were built and then blasted and then built again between wars. She paced back and forth, eyeing the display window boldly, her patience drained. Let them see her. Let them harass. Let them throw potatoes. Let them! Then a flash of movement: the shopkeeper's hand. It opened as swiftly as a bird's wing over the newspaper and snatched it up—the hand, the paper, both of them all at once and then both of them gone, out of sight. Aaseya leaned against the glass, standing on her toes, but she could see no further into the shop.

When he left that morning, Rahim told Aaseya which creek beds he would work. He had a wife who worried about him. He knew this now. It felt easier to let her think he'd be at the shovel, even though he'd be taking pot shots at NGO supply trucks by lunchtime. For weeks, this small crew of workers to which Rahim belonged had been carrying a few greenbacks in their pockets, as paid by the Taliban (by the warlords, by the U.S. Colonels). A system had been worked out, and everyone agreed. This was the job to covet. Besides, the Taliban were paying on time again.

Slow days, Rahim hunched in his foxhole and studied the money, what little of it he earned. The bills—always numbered "1"—smelled like nothing in his own country. He understood "In God We Trust" because the Taliban laughed about it one day when they came down to pay him, jeering at the pyramid eye in mock hypnosis.

"In God, in God," one of them said. He looked high on opium and talked like a rat.

"This is the *real* money," said another. He stood unusually tall. He reached into his shalwar kameez and pulled out a dollar bill, waving it at Rahim and the other men. A crumpled cutout of Osama bin Laden lay pasted over George Washington's head. "In Allah we trust!" the tall one hollered. He laughed when he said it, opening his mouth and flashing a long row of brown teeth.

Rahim resented all of it—the men he worked with, the men he worked for, most days even, the man he saw himself becoming in their presence. But he got along with his partner Badria well enough. For each truck they hassled, they split their pay and, every afternoon, hopped into the back of an old pickup that took them to the edge of town. They always walked the last mile, unsuspected.

Today didn't turn out to be slow. The Americans came. They went on patrol, fanning out at predictable intervals from the Multi National Army Base. They called it "mowing the grass" and treated it as such. Mundane. Ordinary. They'd been here long enough by now, hadn't they? Not much to report anymore, other than the trouble those NGO's experienced, but nothing could be done about that. Nothing with force, at any rate. To the Americans, the Taliban were elusive. In caves. Up the mountain. They hassled the base from afar. They planted explosives. Got high, made plans.

Who knew? They worked at night and didn't have much hold in Tarin Kowt anymore.

Down in the valley, Rahim and Badria baked in the sun along the side of the road, only partially hidden by low shrubs and a shallow foxhole. They watched an armored American military vehicle drive north out of town, then slow to a halt about twenty meters from their hideout. Rahim and Badria stashed their weapons and picked up their shovels. The Americans fired warning shots at the road, then waved the men out.

Rahim faced this once before and had his weapon taken, nothing more. He didn't care about helping the Americans, or the Taliban for that matter. He cared about earning money, about getting all of this over with in as few years as possible, about owning something someday like a home or a shop or anything that could, God willing, belong to him without harassment.

"Put down the shovel," a soldier shouted in English. There were four of them and they were close now, maybe ten meters. The soldier raised his hands in the air, indicating what the men should do. "Put your hands up! Show me your hands! Put your hands up!" If the Americans were anything, they were loud. As though yelling repeatedly could make the words translate mid-air.

Rahim and Badria did as they were shown and stood in the middle of the road, waiting for the four soldiers. When they came close enough, Rahim realized he didn't recognize any of them. He felt relieved; at least these soldiers wouldn't know others from the same base had already pestered him.

"I am on your side," Rahim said in English. It rolled off of his tongue smoothly, just like he'd practiced. "Your side, your side."

"Do you understand English?"

Rahim shook his head, then spoke to the translator who, now

that they stood close, he knew to be the bearded man disguised in American fatigues.

"Why are you here?" the translator asked.

"We're not doing anything wrong. We're digging to make bricks," Rahim said.

"What's he saying?" the first soldier asked.

"They're going to search you," the translator said.

"Fine," Rahim said. "They won't find anything. Let them search us. Tell them they're perverts."

"What's he saying?"

"Search them," the translator said to the soldier. "Search for their wallets, too."

A soldier searched Badria. Another fingered his automatic weapon. The first one, the talker, eyed the situation fiercely.

"How are your children?" Badria said to the translator. "Are they well?" He kept his hands raised as the soldier patted each arm, then his torso, and all the way down each leg.

"How's your mother?" Rahim heckled. "I haven't heard good things about her."

The translator did his best to ignore them.

"Ask them what they're doing on the side of the road," the talker said. "Tell them they're not allowed here."

"You shouldn't be here," the translator said.

"*You* shouldn't be here," Rahim said. Now he was being searched, not roughly but not kindly either. Rahim puckered his lips and considered spitting at the translator's feet, then swallowed hard.

"Ask them what the shovels are for."

"What are you doing here? What are the shovels for?"

"We're digging in the creek bed," Badria said.

"You can't dig here. Don't dig by this highway."

"We'll move," Rahim said.

"What are they saying?"

The translator explained about the digging, and the talker sent two soldiers off the highway to search the foxholes.

In a few minutes, they returned with Rahim and Badria's weapons.

"Ask them where they got the guns," the talker told the translator. He held both weapons in one hand and shook them in Rahim's face. "Ask them why they don't have buckets for their digging, and ask them why they need these guns, and then ask them why they're being lying raghead motherfuckers."

The translator paused, a mental list of words inverting and swapping in his mind until a shorter sentence could be formed. "You're lying," the translator told Rahim and Badria.

"They're clear," the second soldier said. "No more weapons. Just these." He handed two wallets to the talker who immediately sifted through them.

"Ask them where they got these," the talker said and held up the dollar bills.

"From the bazaar," Rahim told the translator. "It's from the soldiers spending their money off base. I don't have to tell you anything. I bought rice. This is my change. Tell that loud one not to touch my money."

"He says it's from the bazaar," the translator told the talker. "He bought rice and this is his change."

"And the guns?"

"Where'd you get the guns?" the translator asked.

"One gun per household," Badria said. "That's the American rule and these are our only weapons. We're following your rules. That's my gun." He nodded at the Russian-era weapon. "The other one is Rahim's."

The talker scribbled Rahim's name down in his notebook.

"I know who you are," Rahim said to the translator, bullshitting. "Does your family know they could be killed?"

The translator made a move to strike. "Your mother is a dog," he shouted. "A dead dog. You don't know me, and you don't know my family."

"What's he saying? Why are you angry?" The talker grabbed the translator's shoulders, holding him back. The other soldiers stepped closer to Rahim and Badria, whose hands were still raised, sweat dripping down their faces in the deadly heat.

"He's an idiot. He knows nothing," the translator barked. "He's threatening me."

"Here we go again," the talker said. "Tell them we're taking their guns. Tell them we'll come back here every hour of every day and that if we find them here again, we'll take them in for questioning. Tell them I don't fucking believe a word they say and that today they are lucky. Tomorrow they might not be."

"We're leaving," the translator told Rahim and Badria. "And we're taking your guns. And if you're seen here again, you'll be shot."

Aaseya's secret could not have been hidden even if she wanted it to be; she felt too eager. Miraculously, the small boy had purchased the newspaper and handed it to her—right there on the sidewalk, in broad daylight. For that brief moment, they could have been the city's bravest citizens or the war's most foolish casualties. In either case, Aaseya took the outdated paper and let the boy keep the change. She all but ran back to the apartment.

Peace talks. City center. Homicide. Business plan. Tribe. Yes, the

English words came back to her with a rash of curiosity. She traced her fingers along each inky line of text, searching for anything familiar. She stopped when she came to a color photograph of a polling center in Iraq. *Vote. Women. Bagdhad.* The Americans were there too, weren't they? It seemed unfathomable to her. She never travelled beyond the small apartment and the few city blocks to the bazaar. How far could the interests of one nation possibly stretch?

"Each word is a link in the chain," an American teacher had told her before the war. She came from the Red Cross or the Peace Corps or some United Christ of Somebody, and she didn't stay long but Aaseya never forgot. "The more words you have, the longer your chain can be." The teacher didn't have much to work with: old textbooks, some flashcards donated by a technical school, dated issues of *National Geographic*. Aaseya horded terms voraciously, the end result a vocabulary of two hundred words, mostly nouns that didn't link together.

She wilted with the realization of how far she had to go. She couldn't do this on her own. The American teacher had been nice enough, but nice didn't add up to sentences; a single word was just a grain of sand. Aaseya wanted a sandstorm, by God, she wanted the entire desert.

What could Rahim say? The only thing he knew for certain was that the Americans took down his name. His first name but his name nonetheless. He and Badria shared the long walk back to town that afternoon, and Rahim weighed his options. He could wait in line outside the Multi National Base each morning, jabbing his way to the front of the crowd and peddling for work. But his name, his face. The base wouldn't take him without an identification card, and he wasn't about to hand that over. He could always return to digging full-time. Not particularly gainful but safer. A little more on the fringes and probably for the better.

By the time Rahim arrived home, later than usual, his mind was made up. Two months. He would stick to full-time digging for two months and then it would be winter and then who knew. For now, it seemed enough. Meantime, Aaseya had already changed scarves twice, prepared a meal, and created a special raisin sauce she felt assured would have the intended effect.

"It's very sweet," Rahim said. He spooned the syrup-drenched halwau politely into his mouth. He rotated his spoon between thumb and pointer finger like a cigar, a gesture more like a general than a laborer, but enough of that. Those years were not discussed.

"I remember reading about molasses," Aaseya said. She took another bite.

"Do you mean at the schoolhouse?" Rahim said.

"Yes. There were five books for our schoolhouse, old Home Economics texts, copyright 1952."

"In English?"

"In English," she said, proudly. "But with enough pictures to make sense. I can't make molasses but I wanted to copy its richness. The dark syrup, at least. I wanted that much." She licked the spoon lavishly, forgetting herself for a moment. That molasses came from sugar hadn't occurred to her. Raisins were dark and sweet and could be liquefied. Molasses was also dark and sweet. Raisins seemed as good a place as any to start.

"Why did they teach you about molasses?"

"They didn't. They taught us math using the measurements in the recipes," she said. "I read the molasses part on my own." She reached for a second helping of halwau. He watched her: the way her hand trembled slightly, the way her lips stayed as tight as a line.

For a breath or two she appeared sheepish.

"Rahim?" She said it like a child, like a beggar. He set his spoon down and looked at her from across the low table. "Rahim, I want to study. There's a business school starting again and a new minister of education and all of this, I think, means good things for us."

"For us?"

Aaseya looked at her husband, not knowing. This could still go either way. She took another bite of the halwau, holding it on her tongue until its sweetness bled down her throat.

"Say more," Rahim said.

Aaseya swallowed. He sounded like her father, that tugging terseness that exhausted her. "What do you want me to say?"

"Say why."

"Because we won't always be at war. Because there have to be more choices. Because all day long there's nothing for me to do, and the other women are proud and busy with their babies. Because there never will be children between us. Because these things are interesting—the books, the stories, the other parts of the world. Because I have ideas. I have so many ideas!"

This was the first she had mentioned babies. Or the lack of them. Moments like this, Rahim felt overwhelmed by the depths of his wife's desires. He understood their marriage was different. He understood about the children because by now there should be some, but there weren't and so he knew. The thought that it could be him was not a thought at all. That Aaseya wanted to talk about babies seemed unnecessary. Yet her ambition for other things provided some measure of relief.

"The studying is fine," Rahim said. "That's all we need to discuss."

She looked at him, sniffling. Terrified. "And the ideas?"

So much still unsettled: the translator could come back, embittered; the new school could open but close within weeks; the war itself could continue another decade or end before the year's first snowfall. But hope seemed just as feasible. That money could be earned without conflict. That an education could be savored.

"*I* have an idea," he said, and he rose from the floor. She stood before he reached her, sliding her hands inside the flaps of his vest. He lifted her, all the parts he knew for certain—her sateen hair, her breasts like two tiny moons, the impossible pink outlining the soles of her feet—and carried her into the bedroom.

By morning, the raisin syrup had hardened like plaster. Aaseya's laughter. Rahim could say he knew that, too.

AWOL

Before going AWOL, I only thought about Canada when that *South Park* movie came out a few years back. "Blame Canada," the cartoon characters jeered. The tune sounded catchy, I remember that much. Otherwise: hockey, maple syrup and a big, cheerful looking flag. That's Canada, right?

Now Canada's the country that took me in. Toronto is the city with organizations for guys like me. And this small block near Withrow Park has become my barracks. A family here lets me stay for free while I sort things out. I don't like to judge. But I don't like being betrayed, either. Whenever I do make it back home to Cleveland, I expect to be laughed at. I never even finished my first tour. Seven months outside Sadr City, then the Army sent me home for a week in November. I never went back.

Mom couldn't feed me enough that visit. Said I looked like a bunch of hungry muscles. Said she oughtta know, she's the one that raised me. I sat down at the Thanksgiving table, feast spread as long as a football field. Dad carved into the eighteen-pound bird, and Uncle Pat started in on the honey-baked ham. I leaned back in my chair, watching the way the meat peeled from the bone. Tender and fatty, like a limb severed by the blast from an IED.

While at home, I got the email from one of the company commanders back in Iraq. They wanted the incident report from 12 NOV 07, paperwork I'd been remiss in filling out for almost two weeks at that point. Right there at my dad's desk, I could feel the heat of Sadr City, its dry dust gathering in my mouth. The way the Iraqis stared at us, running patrol after patrol through their neighborhoods and houses. How their irises looked so dark, when I met civilians gaze-for-gaze I only saw my own reflection, a hundred tiny me's shining back. It made it hard to shake the sight of myself—all that ammo and camo, my tight-lipped expression nothing like the man I wanted to be.

If I filled out the report, I'd have to admit that disobeying my superiors to save lives was an unacceptable infraction. The Army wasn't placing blame. They just didn't want a spoiler like me trying to change the SOP. I'd made it through basic and advanced individual training. Even made it through a heckling captain and, finally, a promotion to Private First Class. But this single-page report that would tidy up a two-hour mission and six dead Iraqis, well, I never responded to the commander's email. Just double-clicked it into the trash along with my tour in Iraq and right then and there started an Internet search to get myself up north.

The Army doesn't search too hard, but I plan to turn myself in for a trial eventually. Me and all our Capitol Hill gurus, the almighty creators of this betrayal. The day those suit coats ante up for crimes against humanity, I'll ante up for AWOL. I can almost see us walking shoulder-to-shoulder through the gates of a military prison. During my hard labor, I'll sweat readily from the work, the life I left in Ohio slowly coming back to me each day I serve my sentence. And the suit coats? They'll work with double the weight on their backs, the ghosts of innocent Iraqis pressing them deeper into the ground.

MRES

The day finally arrived to enter Bagdhad. I remember the sound of our entire brigade crossing the berm, a long, thunderous roll that didn't let up for hours. The sandy terrain caused some trouble for our vehicles. Otherwise, the Iraqi resistance was merely a splinter in the foot of a giant. For every mujahedeen sniper hiding in Saddam Tower, we had entire platoons zeroing in on mission accomplished. When it was all said and done, we surrounded the Al Rasheed Hotel, Presidential Palace, and Ministry of Defense with armored vehicles. The entire city seemed to clamor with one, continuous "Oorah!"

Echo Company regrouped at Saddam International Airport, and our captain radioed his platoon leaders for a chalk talk. Muldrow, Pretty Boy, Thurston, and myself left our men at the main terminal and walked freely to a small departure gate for the meeting. Already, it felt like we owned the place.

Captain Byersdorf had about fifteen years and twice as many deployments to my four years active duty. He also had as much personality as a piece of cardboard. I had yet to see him crack a smile. When and if he spoke, it always sounded labored, the syllables never quite in tact, his tongue tripping over itself. As we approached, I watched him pace between narrow aisles of seating, regarding each empty airport chair like a Marine standing at attention. He moved with impeccable rhythm, his footsteps a slowly clapping metronome. It reminded me of forced piano lessons back in grade school, yet we'd just stormed across the Euphrates River and taken the capital. Byersdorf's stiffness unnerved me.

"It's been a long day, gentlemen," he finally said.

"A long, good day, Sir," Muldrow said. A handful of other platoon leaders nodded in agreement.

Byersdorf stared at us blankly, then stuffed his hands into his pockets. "You've done...well, your men did...What I mean to say is—"

Abruptly, he turned on his heels and led us to a check-in kiosk where he arranged a miniature American flag standing upright in a penholder. Around it sat a stash of desserts and surprise snacks peddled from MREs, a goldmine of selection compared to our usual grab-n-grub daily rations.

"I figured we could—" Byersdorf stopped mid-sentence. He looked at the pile of plastic packages. "I thought our meeting should be a—"

"A celebration, Sir?" Thurston said.

"A ho-down?" Muldrow said.

"A hippy-hippy shake?" Pretty Boy said. We were all amped from combat. It seemed that now, if ever, would be the time to get our Captain to loosen up.

"Call it what you will, gentlemen," Byersdorf said and nodded as he looked at the food cache.

"Thank you, Captain," I said. I spotted a packet of jalepeño cheese spread and reached for it. The other platoon leaders moved in, tearing open vanilla pound cake and Slim Jims, stuffed French toast and lemon poppyseed cake. Byersdorf must have tossed all the Charms aside, catering to our suspicion that Charms bring bad luck. I had to hand it to him; he might have been dogged, but he knew his men.

"It's the little things, isn't it?" he finally said. "I mean, well. You know what I mean, don't you?"

"Yes, Sir!" we said between bites.

"We'll debrief in the morning," Byersdorf said. "But for now, does anyone have questions about the day's events?"

"Well, Sir, as a matter of fact I do," Pretty Boy said. He smiled when he said it, and I knew whatever came next would be a mouthful of smartass. "How many captains does it take to rat fuck a case of MREs?"

Byersdorf rocked back on his heels and considered the inquiry. The corners of his lips twitched into a partial smile or annoyed grimace. Who could tell? I wondered if he even knew we called it that, stealing sweets from everybody's food then using them later for bargaining and rewards.

"I believe I'm unfamiliar with that term," Byersdorf said.

"You mean MRE's, Sir?" said Muldrow.

"No, Muldrow, I mean rat—"

"Because there's lots of names for a Meal Ready to Eat." Muldrow looked at the rest of us, eyes shining.

"Like Mentally Retarded Edibles," Thurston said.

"Or Morsels, Regurgitated, Eviscerated," I chimed in.

"Or Meals Requiring Enema," another platoon leader said.

"Don't forget Massive Rectal Expulsions," Pretty Boy said and tore into his second package of pound cake.

Byersdorf steadied himself against the kiosk, then bent at the waist trying to contain himself. His face turned beet-purple and veins throbbed around his temples. When he straightened back up, his grin looked so wide I could see straight back to his tonsils. The biggest surprise of all? Captain Byersdorf didn't have any teeth.

SIMA COULDN'T REMEMBER

Sima couldn't remember how it started, but something felt wrong. Her husband walked her five miles to a makeshift hospital because they heard a doctor from the UK arrived. She passed out when she got there.

She woke to the smell of her own feces and something else, a mud-soaked, stale scent. A fellow Afghan woman bathed Sima from the bedside: first her feet, then her ankles, then all the way up to the place where something wasn't right. The room felt damp and warm. Several broken beds sat stacked against a wall.

Sima tried to move, but a throbbing sensation shot from her crotch to her heels like one thousand biting spiders. Her stomach felt like a bell without its clapper, a rattle with stones that had turned to dust. When she saw the woman dip a cleansing rag into a bowl of stained water, Sima remembered.

She grabbed the woman's arm and squeezed tightly. They locked eyes for a moment, then Sima brought her fist to her belly and began pounding for the baby she knew she had lost.

"Don't!" the woman said and pinned Sima's forearms to the bed. "There's still the other."

"The other?" Sima froze, lightheaded, her vision a swirling bowl of grain. She exhaled and the woman released her arms.

"Twins," a doctor said, emerging in the doorway. He was white and something else—Sima couldn't tell what—but his Pashtun sounded formal and uncomfortably slow.

"Two?" she asked.

"The first, a boy, is lost," he said. "Six weeks premature. The other has very little chance of survival if it comes too early. You must rest."

The doctor gave Sima steroids that reduced her contractions for two days. Her husband Wasim visited on the third day and paced about the room, tattered sandals scuffing loudly across the floor.

"Will he live?" Wasim asked the doctor.

"Sir? Your wife? I hope so."

"No, the second baby," Wasim said. "Will he live?"

The doctor looked at Wasim quizzically, then told him the truth. "Unlikely."

That evening, Sima awoke to a familiar feeling. Five children already, each so different, yet their signals before birth undeniably exact. She called for assistance and the woman rushed into the room, followed by the doctor.

The woman looked under the sheets between Sima's legs. "Everything is a mess," she said.

It was too soon for the birth but there was fire down there, Sima could feel it. She wanted only to get her baby away from the fire. The doctor moved to help but Sima shook her head, ashamed. Already he had seen more of her own body than she'd seen herself. He monitored from the bedside as the woman assisted. Sima pushed and cried and prayed for nearly an hour, then, very suddenly, the second baby wailed into the night.

"Cover me," Sima said to the woman, then she turned her back to the doctor, sweat-drenched.

When Wasim came the next morning, he wouldn't go into the room. The second baby was a sickly girl. Wasim wanted to yell. He wanted to hit. He wanted to try again and again, God willing, for a son that could bring him pride. Sima heard Wasim in the hallway, insulting the doctor.

"You saved the wrong one," Wasim said. "There are already five girls. We don't need another. What we need is a son."

"You have to leave," the doctor said. "There are patients trying to rest."

Sima opened her eyes and lifted the blankets. A newborn the size of a squash lay nestled in the folds of her breasts. She had saved the baby from the fire, but that was only the beginning. There would be so much more to save her from. Quietly, as though Wasim and the doctor could hear the clamor in her mind, Sima pressed her palm over the baby's face, holding it there until its muscles slackened. When she let go, she felt her daughter back inside of her, pulsing like a tiny ghost, safe inside the walls of her heart.

HOMECOMING

I'm still on the bus. It's taken a long time to get here. We're pulling into the National Guard armory, and between all the flags waving and cameras flashing, I haven't spotted Sarah and our two little girls yet. The windows on the bus are tinted and nobody can see in. The whole town knows who we are though—who made it home, who's never coming back.

I haven't done this before, and I'm not exactly sure how it will figure itself out. But put me in a turret, zeroing in on a slough of insurgents in Saddam Tower, and I know what to do. Drop me into a combat zone with battle rattle and my boys, and sure as hellfire, we'll muscle our way through. To survive, I had to pretend I already died. It made me fight better, imagining I had nothing to lose. It also made me get used to the idea that I'd never see my wife and kids again.

But I can see them now, standing right next to the gigantic AMERICAN HEROES banner. The girls look a few inches taller, brown curls done up in matching pigtails with red, white, and blue ribbons. They cheer with the crowd and point to the bus in anticipation. Sarah's right behind them, so picture perfect it hurts to look. This could be the best it's going to get. My wife. My daughters. They still believe in me.

The bus slows to a stop and the doors open. Before I know it, I'm up and moving with all the guys, tumbling down the steps and whisked into the crowd. That fast, there's Hannah latched around one of my legs and Delphi around the other. Sarah dashes up, then stops, taking us in. I raise my arms, and she slips between them, holding my face in her palms and looking right into me. When I exhale for what feels like the first time in a year, I gaze into her eyes and see a love so fierce and brave, I know she's the real hero among us. My wife. My daughters. The most tender warriors I know.

THE QUIET KIND

Nathan's is the quiet kind of PTSD. Even he knows that much.
Here's one way it works: When teenagers drive past his house on
Grove Road, engines backfiring like the muffled explosions he
heard in the Korengal, he lets his mind make a movie of everything
his cells are telling him to do—Nathan, diving beneath the dinner
table; Nathan, chin-tucked, hands reaching for the safety on his
M4; Nathan, sheepishly returning to his chair, dodging his wife
Tenley's gaze. If he focuses hard enough on the movie, he can keep
still instead, as if he never even heard the *pop-crack*, as if he'd never
even been re-deployed.

There is the Nathan living and the Nathan watching Nathan.
Together, they present a 30-year-old man wound as tightly as the
muscles in his throat. Three weeks out, he's back to full time at
Mountain Hardware, working the six to two. The guys were good
like that—saving his position. He keeps waiting, but they never
ask what he did "over there."

One morning at the shop, an old-timer comes in wearing a
Vietnam Veteran's cap and limping like his right side carries half
a pound of shrapnel.

"What do INS employees do after they get fired?" he calls
over the counter. He holds a bag of Torx head screws in one hand
and some hurricane brackets in the other. Nathan and Ranold, the
Assistant Manager, stare blankly at the vet, who answers his own

joke: "They go work for TSA."

"Good one," says Ranold and drums his fingers on a display case.

"I saw your picture in the paper last month," the vet says to Nathan. "Welcome home."

"Thank you, sir."

"That's a different war over there now, isn't it? GPS units and NVG's. "

Nathan feels the vet's expectant pause. Here is the moment he should say something. Instead, he shrugs and rings up the vet's sale, stuffing the items along with a flyer into a single plastic bag. He came back to work so soon, he reminds himself, because routines feel comforting. Because if he sits alone for too long, his mind spirals toward memories of hand-to-hand combat he has to work hard to undo. He understands now that the idea of coming home is a farce. Nothing seems familiar anymore. No matter what he does, he feels off the mark. Like grabbing for something dropped into a pool and watching how slowly your hand moves, how quickly what you're after starts to sink.

The shop bell rings and the door shuts behind the vet. Nathan reaches for the weekly paper, a ten-page who's who of weddings and obituaries.

"How many tours do you think that guy did?" Ranold asks.

"It's hard to say," says Nathan. "A lot kept going back."

"Like you?"

Nathan stares at the headlines, page two pressed tightly between thumb and forefinger: *Help Your Local Food Pantry, Tigers 2-0 in Pre-Season.* "Yeah, like me. Sort of."

"Well, we're all glad you made it back in one piece," Ranold says. "And you sure look a lot better than that guy."

Nathan forces his gaze away from the paper and out the

storefront windows. He should stand. If he can stand he can talk, and if he can talk he'll be okay. His body obeys, and he sets the paper down lightly, then turns to face Ranold. He will not tell him that making it back in one piece is not the issue, but how many pieces of you got left behind. He will not say that even though he's never been hit, he feels as hollowed as the hemlock trunk on his shooting range. He will, instead, look Ranold in the eyes and speak very, very normally.

"Thanks for saying that," Nathan says, then nods, lips quickly pressing closed.

Maybe it's always been this way. People in the South can claim their reputation of hospitality, but after a decade in Appalachia, Nathan's only ever seen it go skin deep. It keeps him clammed up, backwards from his Midwestern upbringing. He believes in hard love, as his mother puts it, and that's about talking things through even if it means a knock-down drag-out. Eventually, you come out on the other side, and the space around you feels like the cornfields after they're mowed down. Expansive. Open. Ready for a new start. Here in the Blue Ridge, there are too many hollers. Too many places a man can hide.

Nathan has about an hour each afternoon before his daughter Cissy gets home—enough time to grab his rifle and huff ten minutes to the top of the ridge. This particular afternoon, he feels the edge of winter in the fall air. At least he doesn't mind that about the mountains. The way each season teases itself out of the previous, slow and steady until one day you look around and realize the leaves have fallen, the frost turned to snow, your Carhartt vest not quite warm enough anymore. Today's a rag, though. Nathan knows fall will still hang on a few more weeks. He walks quick, gaze up, scanning the trees for variations in the bark. Thick, corrugated bark means hickory. Thin, grey, and blistered means beech. The oaks give him trouble unless the leaves are still on, but he likes the challenge.

Nathan felt uncertain when they first previewed the lot, but up top he found a scar of land about five feet wide and a hundred yards long that opened to the sunlight. He knew he'd need a way to climb from their house at the bottom of the holler, up to the top to get fresh air. The ridgeline would be his place to do it, though he wonders now—how can a man used to endless Indiana pasture ever grow old on land like this? Pin-holed, creek-jambed. Everywhere he looks, ridge after ridge stretches down from high peaks to form a series of claustrophobic hollers. Not too terribly different than the Korengal.

He loads his rifle with few rounds and takes aim. About eighty yards away, an old hemlock has fallen across the ridge, its trunk the width of a man resting sideways on his shoulder, as if taking an afternoon nap. Sunlight warms the bark of the decaying tree, its centerline stripped to the cambium by bullets so that it almost glows. Nathan fires and sees the wood spray. He lowers his rifle and echoes of the single shot sing through the hollers below. The world always feels doubly silent afterwards, a sensation strong enough on most days to remind Nathan how he used to be, if only for an instant, before he starts sinking away from himself again. Sending out a single shot without reply is a luxury lost on most civilians. That's the lure. Perhaps he can normalize himself, he thinks, by repeating this action until both Nathan's—the one living and the one watching—reconcile and let the silence be true.

Anyone would rather forget those night missions, ambushing safe houses deep in the valley with his squad members, not knowing if they'd scare up somebody's children or come around a corner to face a room full of terrorists juiced on heroin. More often it was the latter, and what happened in those dark hallways and leaning shacks had woven into Nathan's muscle memory like a new neuron—ready to fire at the slightest suggestion. He rarely saw their faces, but he could feel their breath—feel it stop once he released his grip or withdrew the blade. He didn't need to know what they looked like; come daylight, the face of any Afghan he saw could have been like the men he'd killed the night before and now here they are, day after day, just on the other side of every blink Nathan takes. Back at the outpost, the imagery almost made sense. Eyes open, he saw Shrouder strapping flea collars around his ankles to keep away the itches, or Babyfat writing his blood type on his combat boots with black Sharpie. Eyes closed, he recalled his first confirmed kill just fifty yards outside the wire, bullet zipping so fast Nathan saw blood and brains splatter out the insurgent's mouth before his own finger came off the trigger. If he didn't see that, he saw Specialist Martin's Humvee, the IED that carved up his fire team like so many sides of beef. Nathan carried severed limbs in a plastic bag over his shoulder, handed them off to Sarge, then retched into the thirsty dirt.

But back home, this movement between worlds is simply too jarring. Eyes open: Cissy with her purple backpack and back-to-school sneakers, jumping into her tall Daddy's arms every day she comes home from school. Or Tenley, the way her lower lip softens whenever he walks into the room, like she still can't believe he made it home uninjured. The contrast alone seems enough to steal a man's breath.

If he and Tenley ever had another child, Nathan would want to talk about making a move. Back to the Midwest. Tenley's parents held Cissy the day she was born. They get to take her for long weekends and see her in dance performances and holiday plays. Nathan's mom drives down twice a year, three times if money is good. It seems only fair to raise a second child closer to the corn. Nathan considers this on his short drive home from Mountain Hardware, passing Coffee Perk, the library, the tackle shop. Main Street even boasts a movie theater now, old church pews salvaged from some place in the Piedmont, then installed in the biggest building downtown. It makes for an odd experience, watching *Avatar* or *Matrix Reloaded* on benches accustomed to prayer.

Outside town, the two-lane highway traces Cane River, mile after winding mile. Ten minutes to Grove Road and another few miles deep into the holler, then home. Before the turn, Nathan passes the park where he and Tenley used to push Cissy on the swings, and when she was smaller, in the stroller along the narrow, looping path. This was their family spot back before Cissy started school, before Nathan's two tours, before they made an offer on their land. Nathan remembers asking Tenley for another child in that park. The day is right there. Cissy had fallen asleep, chin slumped to her neck, rosebud lips partially open. Nathan kept one hand on the stroller, gently rocking it back and forth. His other hand rested on Tenley's knee, and he kept it there to ground himself while he said what he needed to say.

Tenley's response had been practical, financial. As though she felt Nathan's desire quaint. There sat the woman he left Indiana for, the bottle-tanned, blond, smartest person he knew, telling him maybe too much family wasn't the best idea. Her older brother had three kids and "Just look at 'em. Hardly get a moment to themselves." She tilted her gaze toward his, then looked down at the ground. "I'm sorry," she finally said and stood so they could walk back to the car. Tenley had also mentioned money, but Nathan knew there must be more to it than that. Most husbands would resent their wives this privacy, but he can't hold a single corrupted thought about Tenley in his mind. Even on his worst days outside the wire, it had been her photo that kept him believing in the goodness of humankind.

At home, Nathan sets his keys on the counter and aims for the sofa. He doesn't have the energy to hike up to the ridgeline. Not today. He unlaces his work boots and kicks them off and stretches his long body from one end of the couch to the other. When he closes his eyes, sleep isn't far behind.

Cissy can't know that waking Daddy by jostling his toes is not unlike the way his fellow soldiers woke one another for fire watch, but there's something suspicious about her touch. Too light. Too uncertain. Almost as if an insurgent has snuck into the bunkhouse and is standing there, moments before Nathan opens his eyes and sees the tip of an AK targeting his forehead. First response: every muscle in his body cinches tight, right up to the air trapped inside his lungs. Nathan realizes almost immediately how horribly this could go—Cissy feeling Daddy toss her to the ground with the flip of his legs, then his chest slamming into hers as he readies for the chokehold, then no—wait. It's just his daughter. His only daughter.

Nathan opens his eyes and sees her there, blond pigtails and a toothy grin. "Sweetie, come on up here, away from Daddy's feet, okay?" He might be whispering. The Nathan watching Nathan can't be certain.

She slips her backpack off her shoulders and curls into Nathan's arms. He shifts to his side so he can cradle her there, his little turtle. He wonders if she feels his heart thumping through his chest wall or his lungs cinching tighter, his consciousness holding court in a violent world.

"How was school today?" he asks. He's back inside himself

now, the good father on the sofa with his girl. He wants to cry at the simplicity of it. Tenley would like to walk in on this. He aches at the thought of his wife, feels a clutching of energy below his belt. He needs her. To know she needs him back. When he came home the second time, he felt cut down. Tenley and Cissy faired so well without him. They missed him, surely. But didn't they need him while he was gone, too? Weren't there things besides cleaning gutters and water bars that only he could provide? Nathan doesn't feel certain anymore.

He squeezes Cissy between his arms and lets out a sigh. She's saying something. Her day. That's right. Nathan strains to focus, her voice so sweetly syncopated he could almost forget everything else. "Let's get up, my girl. Let's see what you've got for homework."

For Tenley's part, Nathan isn't so much divided in two as he is an anomaly. She makes a study of him—this man she knows wholly, though now it seems an entire continent of unknowns could live inside of him. If a map existed, she might hesitate to look. Since his return, it's one day at a time—a stark contrast to the dreaming and planning they did before his first deployment. There had even been talk of another child once, but how could Tenley have explained? She often thinks of having a larger family, but only in the way she thinks about what might be cooked for dinner or what movie might be showing that weekend. She certainly doesn't think about children in a bodily way. She's known one was enough since she was a child herself playing house with the neighborhood girls, always insisting on a small, pretend family. What would she and Nathan do with a new baby, anyway? Tenley sees enough of life's miracles and failures at work as a CNA. Clocking out is perhaps her favorite part of the day. That and coming home to see Nathan there, for good.

She imagines their house sealed tightly from the rest of the world, the only place in the Blue Ridge her Nathan feels safe. He cried every day that first week home, and not the kind of crying that could be stopped. Crying in the hallway, crying while sitting in the truck in their driveway, crying over his first home-cooked meal. Crying with deep, body sobs Tenley hoped might bring the rest of her husband back to her. "Is there more?" she asked and pressed his wet face between her palms. She even held him a few nights in the beginning, opposite how they used to sleep: Tenley's body cupped along Nathan's back, her arm slumped over his shoulders, barely reaching halfway around. It made her feel uncertain, like borrowing someone else's high heels. For so long she prayed to have Nathan standing in their living room dressed in civilian clothes, dimpled-smile across his face. Now that she has him, she knows she should have prayed for more.

But after that first week, Nathan's crying stopped. Safe meant silent, and Tenley worked to make their house the place Nathan wouldn't be pressed to explain himself, the place where, if they all worked at it, he wouldn't even have to remember Afghanistan at all. Slowly and deliberately, he amputated memories. Tenley knew enough to feel it happening but had no clue how to make it stop—or if she should. She watched Nathan hunker down as if riding out a storm. If he spoke at all, his words came between sharp inhalations of breath. Even still, Tenley occasionally caught herself wishing Nathan would lose his temper. If he could just get pissed about something, she might be able to angle back into him, back to the way things used to be.

Tenley's handling of Nathan's return might look cold to anyone on the outside peeking in. That's the thing about small Southern towns, as much as she loves them. Even her closest girlfriends dish judgment, warning her about the way combat changes a man. As if they know. As if they wore body armor, marveled at bullet holes through Kevlar, and lived on MREs for almost a year. Not that she did, but she's closer to it than any of them and by holiday season, just when everyone hosts parties and cook-offs, she can almost scream she so desperately needs a break from all the social saccharine. The house transformed into a vacuum and now here she is, suggesting a two-week vacation at her mother-in-law's on a landscape so barren she feels the wind might blow her all the way to Canada.

"Do you want to?" Tenley asks. She's been prepping pork roast since mid-afternoon: marinating, stuffing, considering side dishes. Sunday dinner is her favorite, and with Cissy tall enough to see over the countertops, she has a little helper.

"Let's go see Grandma!" Cissy grins when she says it, leaping into her mother who in turn bumps a pan of steaming green beans. Water hisses onto the stove.

"Everything alright in there?" Nathan calls from the living room where he sits, hunched over a Scrabble board.

"Nothin' doin'," Tenley calls. "My turn yet?"

"You're not going to like this," Nathan says. He walks into the kitchen.

"Triple score?"

"Double. But I used a Q and added to your last word."

"Ditch?"

"Yeah. Sorry, baby." He catches her around the waist as she moves to walk past. She loves that. How his wide palms make her feel petite. But she doesn't like the other things those hands might have done. She slides quickly from his touch. That's another thing they haven't found their way back to, either. But enough—Tenley hasn't even told her girlfriends as much. It's smarter to let them guess. Chances are they'll conjure a better version.

Tenley walks to the table. "QUIDDITCH?" she calls. "That's not a word."

"It's Harry Potter's game, Mama. And it's a word." They all stand in the living room, encircling the game board. Cissy flips through the Scabble dictionary. "Here, Daddy," she says, proudly opening to the Q section. "Can you find it?"

"Let's see…" He slowly thumbs through the pages.

"Mama says we're going to Indiana for Christmas!" say Cissy. "She says maybe even for two weeks."

Nathan glances at Tenley from across the table. "Two weeks, huh?"

"It would make your mother so happy," she says. If she could just be direct, she'd like herself a little more. Her husband is home safe. She should be happy. And yet she has to re-learn him. Lately, she resents it. Nathan does things he doesn't realize—little shouts in his sleep, nightly twitches and jerking. He even developed a new mannerism, a sideways lizard-stare that makes him look half-in and half-out of conversations. She can't tell him. How could she? He's been through enough. If she can get him back home, maybe he'll remember himself. Indiana. The one thing, she used to tease, he might have married instead of her.

"Do you mean it, Ten?"

"I do." She holds his gaze when she says it, marking the promise.

"I remember those two words," Nathan says, and when Tenley blushes into a smile the family looks, for a moment, like a combat zone never came between them.

Winter now, and Nathan zips his coat to his chin, heading for the ridgeline. He follows his narrow footpath through the browned leaves, flecks of mica glittering atop the soil. He hopes the cold front is just that and won't bring precipitation. Tomorrow they hit the road for Indiana. His mother called twice that week already, asking what more she could prepare, oh and didn't I tell you? Your sisters are coming! She hadn't said it, but Nathan knows that means nieces, nephews, and brothers-in-law as well. He tries to feel excited but suddenly what seemed like it would be an easy Christmas—maybe the one he'll finally be able to convince Tenley they should make the move—will now be a hustle-bustle negotiation of shared bathrooms and chips 'n' dip.

Up top he hears the wind hiss, a few territorial squirrels yakking over their stashes. In the Korengal the monkeys made that racket, screaming day and night without reason. Memories of their cries are still one of the few things Nathan hasn't been able to sever. Even now, monkeys chatter through his nightmares. He hikes a little further and considers shooting the squirrels but decides against it. He never liked killing. Until joining the Army, he never realized that what a man believes could be so far from what a man does. Nathan aims at the hemlock trunk and fires. Now, he has to live with parts of himself he hates—and the unsettling fact that those are also the parts he misses most. Combat, that dopamine-crazed brotherhood where every move matters. He can't remember the last time he did something bearing that much consequence for his own family. Life pales in comparison to the constant threat of death.

Nathan loads two more rounds and fires, the sound like somebody slapping cupped hands over his ears. It feels good. He fires again, then walks to the target. The old trunk has nearly rotted through in several places, a few bullet-ends are visible in the mealy heartwood. He perches against the edge of the widest section and stuffs his hands into his pockets, fingers curling around the spare bullets like loose change. How many bullets did he dodge in the Korengal? In truth, the ones he didn't dodge scared him more. The ones he never knew came so close. That was the rub, wasn't it? You could dodge one just to get sliced open by another. Or worse, the one you dodged might spiral through a fellow squad member instead. He slides a bullet from his pocket and slips it into his mouth. The taste of metal startles: cold brass beneath his hot tongue. Nathan's thoughts race. For a while he imagines the smell of the outpost (how strange to miss something so rank). He remembers the piles of rocks for protection, the rations of salt tablets, the buzz of firefights. He rolls the bullet around in his mouth, metal clicking against his teeth. Few people can understand this kind of longing. He can. His wife Tenley cannot. And there it is, that first, cracking admission of her imperfection. He feels relieved.

That night, after they tuck Cissy in and start the last load of laundry before the big drive, Nathan decides he will try to talk. He can't be certain what he'll say, but he knows if he starts by telling Tenley about antics his platoon pulled during the weeks of boredom between missions, he'll stumble into a tale and maybe they can both laugh. Tenley can't understand, but she can listen, and Nathan knows he owes her that chance. He mutes the television when he hears her step down the hall. She walks into the bedroom. He hasn't looked at her closely in months but he looks now. The best surprise is this: she hasn't changed. Thin tank top, flannel pants, and a slightly knock-kneed gait that makes her hips look wider in the best possible way. Even the curves of her elbows appear smooth, the dip of her collarbone, the way her hair (finally down at the end of the day) teases the tops of her shoulders. She shuts the door and crawls into bed. When Nathan doesn't move to turn off the bedside light, she turns to him, questioning.

His throat collapses. This won't work. He moves his lips to her instead.

Back before they were who they are now—seventeen-year-olds working their first time away from home as counselors for a summer camp in Virginia, Nathan offering Tenley his class ring after just eight weeks—neither could have guessed themselves into this house, this bedroom, these nervous hands now fumbling with clothing, the sheets, the goddamn comforter. Nor could they have guessed what came so easily then is now a quietly suffered re-education. Tenley works on her mind, hard. Considers turning off the light, the television. She will not think of the fifteen hundred million ways her husband might have killed another human being, fingers on a trigger, fingers in her hair. She closes her eyes and pushes back at Nathan but doesn't let go. She knows this. His smell. The heat of him. She finds herself on top and presses her hands into his chest; moves with him. If this is suffering, she wants more.

Nathan moves with her, but soon his mind splits, the Nathan watching Nathan getting in the way. He kicks his legs, forces his eyes open. He will not lose this moment. *Look at her. Look at her.* The first time he ever thought he'd been hit, he hadn't wished for anything. Just laid there, face-planted in the middle of an IED-laden road, and marveled at the blankness. Later, he felt ashamed. Shouldn't he have thought of his wife? His daughter? He heard someone holler for a medic and that's when he realized he was clean. The blast knocked him out but didn't cut him up. He crawled his way to the medic and hollered: "I'm out of ammo, but I'm not hit." The medic handed him a magazine with one hand and kept firing with the other.

Tenley repositions her hips and slides her hands up Nathan's chest toward his throat. Not a choke but something reminiscent in an accidental sort of way. The Nathan watching Nathan could have told her not to do that but she wouldn't have heard, she was in it. Now it's too late and Nathan hooks his hands around her wrists, angling his legs so he can flip out of the attack, every cell in him arguing: *No! Yes!* Tenley seizes the half-second before disaster and opens her eyes.

"Nathan!" She says it loud and he loosens his grip.

That fast, she slaps him across the face, and the house holds still. One breath, two breaths. Three. They stare at each other, chests heaving, and Nathan can almost taste it—the freshness of something new breaking into him as something old sinks away. Just then, he laughs out loud.

They stay up most of the night after that—Nathan talking, Tenley listening, both of them finding each other again like that first summer. When Cissy tiptoes into their bedroom at half past eight the next morning, she can't know that in nine months, she'll have a baby brother. Nathan and Tenley can't know either, but it won't be long. Cissy scoots on top of the covers and noodles into her mother's arms, pink nightgown damp with warmth from the night before.

"Mama, it's time to go," she whispers.

Tenley curls around her daughter and feels her body, toasty as a furnace. "I know, darlin'," she says. "Did you sleep okay?"

"I dreamed that Santa brought me an iPod for Christmas," Cissy says, excited now. "And also a jewelry box and tap shoes and a trampoline for the backyard."

"Lucky girl," Nathan says. He rolls onto his side and drapes his arm over Tenley, hand reaching all the way to Cissy's shoulder. "Guess we'd better let Santa know you already got everything you wanted, no need to come find us in Indiana."

"It was a dream, Daddy."

"A good one, too." He smiles. He feels suddenly shy, recalling the night before. But shy is better than shut down. He could almost get used to it. "Sweetie, go and brush your teeth so we can get dressed, okay? I'll toast us some waffles while Mama's in the shower."

Cissy skips out the door. Nathan presses his nose into the back of Tenley's neck, inhaling in her scent. He knows there's work ahead, but he has to believe a small hurdle has been cleared. Tenley turns to kiss him, then slides from the bed and walks into the bathroom.

After waffles there's the rest of the packing, setting the faucets to drip in case of a storm, stopping the mail, and one last errand in town. But by lunchtime they hit the Interstate and by mid-afternoon cross into Kentucky. They'll be late arriving, but it doesn't bother Nathan. He calls home and talks to his sisters for a minute, then tells his Mom to have everybody go ahead with dinner. They're staying two whole weeks. There's plenty of time. Besides, he doesn't want to rush this: cruising along at sixty, a mirror-full of mountains in the rearview, the horizon opening more and more with every mile.

EPILOGUE

As I worked on this book, people often asked why I wrote about war. The wars in Iraq and Afghanistan were described as "my generation's," but I knew very little about them and had no immediate ties to the military. Right or wrong, "their" side or "ours," I wanted to know, on the level of basic human experience, what were these wars actually like? How did people operate under extreme conditions with less-than-ideal tools for survival? How did their personal traits influence their motivations and experiences against the backdrop of war? What were the impacts of war inside the family home or in the far reaches of an individual's mind?

I wanted to write my way toward answers to these questions by considering the intimate moments of a soldier's or civilian's life. Images, decisions, and thoughts so small and experienced under such strain that even an interview with the most forthcoming individual could not unearth them. I was not interested in becoming an embedded reporter or detailing the facts of either war through journalism. There are many writers who have done that and done it well. As someone inclined to make sense of the world through story, I knew my window into these wars would have to be narrative. What better way to begin than with unanswered questions and the creative freedom to write my way toward something I could believe.

As I researched and imagined, inspiration for stories in

Flashes of War initially came in two ways: from the rhythmic and emotional quality of a quote or from the jarring contrast of a memorable image. One example is a series of YouTube videos I watched with embedded reporter Ben Anderson. In an interview, a soldier looked into the camera and said, "America's not at war. America's at the mall." I felt struck by the tension and cadence of this—the war versus the mall—and wrote my first war story titled, "While the Rest of America's at the Mall." Another example came from the movie *Kandahar*, which included a scene depicting a group of Afghan civilians, each missing a leg and using crutches. The men raced toward a plane flying overhead that dropped half a dozen prosthetic legs from its hatch, sending them down on parachutes. When I saw this, I paused the DVD. The countryside looked beautiful: rolling brown hills against a cloudless, azure sky. Then there were these legs silhouetted against the sun, these men hobbling toward them. This was a moment my mind could not comprehend, and I felt compelled to explore it by writing "Amputee" and "My Son Wanted a Notebook."

To help immerse myself in the environment of war, I plastered my studio walls with quotes and photos. I used Google Images to "visit" Iraq and Afghanistan. In almost all cases, I was able to intersperse the stories with real locations, accurate historical or cultural references, and current facts. I read books and watched countless hours of movies until the wars found their way into my dreams. I looked up weapons, order of military rank, Arabic and Pashtun terms, colors of uniforms. The list of new phrases at my disposal seemed endless: fobbits, ripped fuel, hot brass, haji, raghead, yalla yalla, got your six, pressin' the flesh, stay frosty. Likewise, primary accounts from civilians proved evocative: "Since my brother was killed, I cannot taste my tea. I cannot taste anything;" "I am but one fistful of dirt;" "There is no law. The gun is law."

Eventually, I filled myself with enough information to precisely imagine my way toward fiction I could believe in. I certainly didn't have all the answers, but I felt the stories brought me closer to something real and, if nothing else, could bear witness to the complexity of hope and suffering.

INTERVIEW WITH
THE AUTHOR

Katey Schultz in conversation with Patricia Ann McNair.

While writing much of *Flashes of War*, her spectacular debut story collection, Katey Schultz was on the road. For three years, she traveled from place to place, settling long enough to enjoy a writer's residency here, a fellowship there, and a teaching gig wherever she could. Katey now makes her home in a vintage Airstream in North Carolina, but the trailer is stationery; a place to rest for a while, and to write.

Recently, Katey Schultz spent time with me talking about *Flashes of War*, the concept of home, the language of war, writing flash fiction, and a whole lot of other things. Here then, is a bit of our conversation:

PMc: Much of this book was written while you were on the road, moving from place to place, in temporary housing, away from your own home. Do you think your own experience of being relatively "homeless" has influenced your writing of these stories in which people are driven from their homes, are dropped into places that are not their homes, and are returned to the homes that are no longer the places they remember?

KS: I do think that being "homeless" while I wrote *Flashes of War* influenced the work, but I'm not sure it was in the ways that you suggest. I can say, however, that there are several stories where a sense of longing for the familiar is pervasive. In "Getting Perspective," Lillis struggles to identify herself and relate to her surroundings in the absence of her husband. In "The Quiet Kind," Nathan misses home so badly, the implication is that he loves Indiana as much as (or perhaps more than) his own wife. In "Deuce Out," Stephanie takes loyalty to her brother to an extreme, no matter the cost.

I think the feverishness of some of the situations these characters face was informed by my own impatience to get wherever I was trying to go as I journeyed from state to state, writing gig to writing gig. Where was I going? To actual, physical places—sure—but I was also on a more metaphorical path of my own self-discovery as a writer, learning how far I could push myself creatively and financially in order to make a life doing what I love.

PMc: I wonder what it was like to carry these stories with you as you traveled. I imagine you had to find a way to reinsert yourselves into these fictional lives each time you came to a new place. Hours on the road likely allowed you the opportunity to write in your head or think about the stories and the book; but did you create a new writing space in each new place? And did you appoint it populated with things related to your work and research?

KS: Whenever possible, I tried to complete a draft of a story before moving on to another residency, for exactly the reasons that you suggest. Getting back into a story, both mentally and in terms of my research notes, always took some time. This meant that, for the most part, I was only ever working on one story at a time until I could bring it to a satisfying first draft or conclusion.

For many of the stories, and especially for the flash fiction pieces such as "MIA," "WIA," "KIA," "AWOL," and "MRE" that all came from a loose contextual theme, yes, I did recreate my writing space each new place that I went. For three years, my surroundings were constantly in flux. I frequently forgot what season it was, having gone from a severe Texas drought, to a picturesque fall in the Shenandoah foothills, to a winter on the edge of an island in the North Pacific Ocean in a matter of three months, for example. I had to keep something constant and, other than the act of writing itself, that constant became the war notes, photos, and magazine cutouts I hung on my walls each new place that I went.

I kept a long sheet of butcher paper that listed Afghanistan colors, physical land features, and cultural objects and taped that to the wall. I kept another for Iraq. Likewise, lists of possible scenes and locations (such as the Multi National Army Base in "The Ghost of Sanchez" or the camps at al-Hadra in "Refugee"), printouts of Google satellite images detailing downtown Baghdad or rural Arkansas ("Home on Leave"), and links to YouTube videos detailing head-cam footage of U.S. soldiers being ambushed ("While the Rest of America's at the Mall"). I often looked at images of Afghan children in school or orphaned on the streets ("My Son Wanted a Notebook"), members of the Taliban with their guns raised ("Aaseya & Rahim"), soldiers hooked up to IVs ("Amputee") or working drills in basic training ("Deuce Out"). Surrounded by these things, I could move around in my homemade theatre of war, so to speak, and create new characters and stories no matter where I found myself. When it was time to move on, I folded everything up and fit it into a single file folder and repeated the entire "nesting" process for my writing space at the next stop.

PMc: Past wars were more obviously reported (complete with many images) in mainstream media than these current wars seem to be. It was not unusual for the nightly news on any network to show footage of combat and its aftermath during the Vietnam War; images from the atrocities of WWII were in all of the newspapers and shown in news trailers at the cinema. While the images from today's wars are available on-line and in other places, it can take some searching to get any sort of accurate picture of what is really happening. Did the absence of easily accessible information affect your desire to tell these stories?

KS: Sixteen years ago, I made a conscious decision to live my life without television. Since that time, I have occasionally kept up with the news through NPR and BBC radio broadcasts, or subscriptions to the print editions of *The Week* and *The New York Times*. Perhaps because of this, I was doubly separated from even the mainstream coverage being offered about these wars. I didn't see footage of the two planes flying into the World Trade Center until a week after 9/11. I found out about Osama bin Laden days after he was killed. All of which is to say, I guess, that I'm not the best judge of what is "easily accessible" information and what isn't—because I've consciously chosen to remove myself from very large parts of mainstream or popular culture.

But your question about what affected my desire to tell these stories is a good one, and for me, I suspect that it has more to do with a sense of justice than anything else. I had been told that the wars in Iraq and Afghanistan were "my generation's." This confused and interested me, as I did not feel a part of them in any way, although I very much wished that we could resolve our conflicts without going to war. So my desire sprung, in part, out of a sense of duty to understand what going to war could possibly mean, and furthermore, to understand something that was being called "mine." I needed to get at the human component of war, and in order to do that, I had to dig much deeper than anything the media was offering me. I pushed my research to a certain point, and then I let imagined stories take over.

The more I wrote, the more I realized that you can never really point a finger at the starting point of war, nor can you blame one side or one person any more than another. The causes and conditions that create war seem so intricate and complex, that no matter what angle I took through fiction, the answers were never going to be direct or without realistic, complicated implications. That's rich terrain to explore when it comes to narrative, because there are countless outcomes and layers and each one is pertinent. So my job became not only to explore these possibilities, but to do so with heart and accuracy.

PMc: Let's talk about form and structure for a bit. You have long been actively engaged in writing the very short-short story, commonly known as "Flash Fiction." Why did you choose this form to tell so much of this book? And how did the longer stories evolve from this collection of otherwise brief pieces?

KS: At first, I had to write flash fiction because I didn't know enough about Middle Eastern culture or 21st Century warfare to sustain longer narratives. Also, I feel that the snapshot stories are very indicative of what actual war and survival must be like. We often remember intense situations in flashes or moments, our senses heightened. In this way, the flash fiction form lent itself perfectly to the backdrop of war.

Through research, inquiry, and imagination I was eventually able to wrap my brain around enough details to feel confident imagining fictional, yet realistic, people and places. A well-rounded character needs quirks, needs to suffer or struggle, needs to have desires and hopes, and needs to be able to react convincingly in full scene. In turn, a full scene needs to happen in a thought-out setting—one that is culturally and physically accurate, as well as one that provides triggers for characters to react to and against, thus moving the narrative along.

It took over a year of writing about war before I felt I was able to successfully move believable characters around in believable places for more than four pages or so. When that time came, I wrote "Deuce Out" after talking with a few soldiers at a recruitment office in northern Michigan regarding the steps for enlistment. Next came "Aaseya & Rahim," which I wrote near Fairbanks, Alaska, where I had a writing friend who was a former war correspondent. Then came "The Ghost of Sanchez," which I wrote during a two-week solo stint in a cabin in Denali. These three stories rely heavily on the technical, but once I gained momentum, I was able to dig deeper into character as well. That's when stories like "Getting Perspective" and "The Quiet Kind" came, and onward I went. I enjoyed being able to pay more attention to things like moral decisions, changes of heart, backstory, deep symbolism, and extended metaphor. Those are all craft elements I care very much about, and because I had refined my use of language at the line-level to write so many of the flashes, by the time I got to the longer stories, the word choice and basic facts of each piece came to me naturally—freeing me up to focus on the bigger stuff.

PMc: You mention language. In past conversations about the book, you have said that part of what drew you to the topic of war was that the contemporary language of war had become part of everyday use--particularly among your young students who have lived most of their lives while the United States has been at war. In some stories, it seems as though language (this "new" language of war included) helps drive the story movement. Can you talk some more about your attention to language and word choice in the stories? Do you have specific examples of stories in which you are aware of this attention?

KS: While I will always love reading or hearing a well-told story, I'll always love trying to write one even more. For me, it is a physical and chemical process that begins with individual words, then builds into something with a compelling narrative. I get pretty jazzed about using new words because, in order to do so convincingly, I have to create believable characters and places that allow me to put those words into action. I've often said that giving a writer a new word is like giving a painter a new shade of green. Once you know it exists, it's darn near impossible to carry on without using it.

You're absolutely right about language driving the narrative in parts of this book. Sometimes, that came out in rather technical considerations, such as describing the "hero mission" in "The Ghost of Sanchez." I read somewhere that a "hero mission" is when surviving U.S. soldiers have to recover the body of a fellow soldier killed in action. I felt intrigued by that language and the connotations behind it. In order to tap into that intrigue and write the scene, I had to understand how convoys moved, how a bridge might be ambushed, and how Marines might rappel down to the water. So in that particular case, my interest in using the word and tapping into the implied emotions behind it, led directly to an action scene in a story.

In other stories, my attention to language and word choice felt much more rhythmic and organic. "They Call Us Cherries," "While the Rest of America's at the Mall," and "My Son Wanted a Notebook" are a few examples of this. A "cherry" is like a rookie; a soldier who has never been to battle. We all know that "cherry," in more frequent slang, also refers to a woman who is a virgin. The word took on dual meaning, then, as it was taken from one put down of women and transferred to a put down for new soldiers (of any gender). For this reason, I felt it had a lot of power and I wanted to explore that on the page. When I started to write the story, however, the emotion took over. The final piece is more of a dramatic monologue that is driven forward by the repetition and cadence of an entire litany of specific, aggressive speech or snapshots.

PMc: This precision and attention to language in connection with dramatic scene, story, and story movement must affect your revision process as well. Would you mind talking about that some?

KS: When I'm revising flash, I get pretty surgical. I lean most heavily on my verbs, because they are the only part of speech we have to move a story forward. Verbs are action, all stories need action, therefore in flash especially, the verbs better be pulling their weight because there is only so much space to get the job done. In "Amputee," for example, the tall day lillies "wave their petaled hands in the breeze." Every word there matters to Becca, whose own hand is missing and will never wave again, so in that line you have the verb ("wave") and the noun ("hands") really working double-time. Or in "Into Pure Bronze," when the sky over Kabul Stadium looks "star-pocked." "Pock" is a bit more aggressive than, say, "twinkle." Creative decisions like that matter, whether they happen in first drafts or later on in revision, because the individual words add up over the course of a story to imply deeper meaning.

After zeroing in on my verbs (and sometimes the nouns that they refer to), I look at unnecessary words—fillers that destroy rhythm or get in the way of urgency—and I cut those out. Finally, I consider voice, which is where a lot of my stacked adjectives, use of slang, or decisions about punctuation come into play.

In terms of scene, I'm a big fan of clarity. I want to know when something starts and when it ends. There's no time in flash to wait for the reader to figure things out. That being said, you've always got to be a beat or two ahead of the reader, because part of the momentum of flash fiction stories is dependent upon on the reader's own experience of putting things together as the story unfolds on the page. So I try to be clear where it matters—scene, time, physical movement—but I'm plenty confident being creatively unclear where it matters as well. For example, the opening line in the first story of the book, "While the Rest of America's at the Mall," starts readers en medius res: "It's not quite sniper fire but it isn't random, either." What does "it" refer to? My copyeditor got all over me for that, and rightly so (in a way), because how can you start a book with a pronoun that doesn't refer clearly to a noun that hasn't been mentioned yet? But the move is effective, I think, because it both realistically conjures the surprise elements of warfare while also jump-starting the story as it gives the reader just enough of a clue to realize we're off and running.

When it came time to revise less traditional stories, such as "They Call Us Cherries" or "The Waiting" (both parts), I understood that these were more of a glimpse into a world of energy and ideas, and less about being able to pinpoint any particular character in a lasting time or place. I decided to keep them in the collection because I felt they captured a certain mentality or general experience that is universal to the culture of any war, in any country, across any decade.

PMc: I imagine it would be difficult to leave these characters with whom you have lived for quite some time. Are any of them still in your head, giving you more stories to tell?

Earlier, we were discussing the ways in which I reinserted myself into the lives of my characters as I moved from place to place. Although it's true that I frequently finished a story before I had to pack up and leave, there were two stories in particular that were different. Those were: "The Quiet Kind" and "Aaseya & Rahim." I can tell you where and how I was sitting when I wrote the opening pages to "The Quiet Kind" (propped up on two pillows in a stiff-backed chair at Madroño Ranch in south-central Texas) and "Aaseya & Rahim" (in a derelict steel, swiveling office chair tucked into the corner of an off-the-grid, hike-in-only, rustic cabin near Fairbanks, Alaska).

I remember this because I think some part of me knew that I had stumbled upon characters that were going to make me work really hard for them, and I felt invigorated by that challenge. For days after starting these stories, my world shrunk to just a few square feet: the distance between my hands and the keyboard, my computer and my research notes, and my desk and the bathroom. I felt if I strayed too far mentally or physically, I'd lose them. Later, during those long driving days or flights and layovers, I was able to conjure the intimacy of that foundation for each of these stories and roll ideas around in my head—sometimes writing, other times just considering the ins and outs of what made Nathan tick, or what Aaseya's innermost desires were.

As it turns out, these two stories feature characters who now appear in my novel-in-progress. Nathan is the main character, with numerous appearances from Aaseya and Rahim, and a few mentions of Tenley. The entire novel takes place in one day, set in the imagined village of Imar, in the real province of Oruzgan, Afghanistan.

PMc: Thanks, Katey Schultz, for this insight into this very fine story collection. I am eager to read more from you.

Patricia Ann McNair is the author of the award-winning story collection The Temple of Air. *For more information:*
www.PatriciaAnnMcNair.com

READER'S GUIDE

1.   Discuss the variety of meanings of the words *flash* and *war* in the book's title, *Flashes of War*.

2.   The collection consists of twenty-four pieces of flash fiction and seven longer short stories. What defines flash fiction? Compare and contrast a story such as "Home on Leave" or "The Quiet Kind" with "They Call Us Cherries" or "Homecoming." These stories have similar elements, but the first two are short stories, and the second two are flash fiction. How does that difference affect your response as a reader?

3.   Author Katey Schultz has no direct, personal experience with war or connection to the military and has never been to the Middle East. What are examples of details in her narration and dialogue that make her fiction realistic? In the epilogue, Schultz explains of her research for this book, "Eventually, I filled myself with enough information to precisely imagine my way toward fiction I could believe in." Consider the roles research and preciseness play in creativity.

4.   Authors and their editors carefully curate the order of stories in a collection of fiction. Consider the order in *Flashes of War*. What tone does the opening story, "While the Rest of America's at the Mall," set for the rest of the book? Why does it matter that

"WIA," "MIA," and "KIA" come one right after the other and in the order they do? How would your lasting impression of the book be different had "My Son Wanted a Notebook" instead of "The Quiet Kind" ended the collection?

5.   Why is "The Waiting" split into two separate stories but labeled as two parts of the same story?

6.   While writing a collection of such diverse voices, Schultz has said that she found it easiest to speak from the American male perspective. Why do you find it surprising or not that a female author would feel this?

7.   Just as a collection of short stories is curated for order, it's curated for content. Schultz wrote but ultimately decided not include a story told from the perspective of an Iraqi suicide bomber and another about an American contract truck driver delivering goods to US Army bases in Afghanistan. Though you know little about these two stories, what are some reasons you can imagine that she made this choice? How might the book, and your reaction to it, be different had those stories been a part of it?

8.   Those who go off to fight wars are still usually male, and those who are left to keep the home fires burning are usually female. In the Middle East, everyday society is heavily segregated by sex. Does this book about situations divided by sex speak more to male or to female readers and why?

9.   Ultimately, is this a book of hope or of despair? Of caution or of celebration?

ABOUT THE AUTHOR

Katey Schultz grew up in Portland, Oregon, and is most recently from Celo, North Carolina. She is a graduate of the Pacific University MFA in Writing Program and recipient of the Linda Flowers Literary Award from the North Carolina Humanities Council. She lives in a 1970 Airstream trailer bordering the Pisgah National Forest. This is her first book.

Please visit: www.kateyschultz.com

Apprentice House is the country's only campus-based, student-staffed book publishing company. Directed by professors and industry professionals, it is a nonprofit activity of the Communication Department at Loyola University Maryland.

Using state-of-the-art technology and an experiential learning model of education, Apprentice House publishes books in untraditional ways. This dual responsibility as publishers and educators creates an unprecedented collaborative environment among faculty and students, while teaching tomorrow's editors, designers, and marketers.

Outside of class, progress on book projects is carried forth by the AH Book Publishing Club, a co-curricular campus organization supported by Loyola University Maryland's Office of Student Activities.

Eclectic and provocative, Apprentice House titles intend to entertain as well as spark dialogue on a variety of topics. Financial contributions to sustain the press's work are welcomed. Contributions are tax deductible to the fullest extent allowed by the IRS.

To learn more about Apprentice House books or to obtain submission guidelines, please visit www.apprenticehouse.com.

Apprentice House
Communication Department
Loyola University Maryland
4501 N. Charles Street
Baltimore, MD 21210
Ph: 410-617-5265 • Fax: 410-617-2198
info@apprenticehouse.com
www.apprenticehouse.com